Crossroads

Crossroads

MACHON MALKA MIRTZA

ISRAEL BOOKSHOP
Publications

M. JAKUBOWICZ

Copyright © 2014 by Israel Bookshop Publications

ISBN 978-1-60091-311-2

Book design by Elisheva Appel

Distributed by:
Israel Bookshop Publications
501 Prospect Street / Lakewood, NJ 08701
Tel: (732) 901-3009 / Fax: (732) 901-4012
www.israelbookshoppublications.com / info@israelbookshoppublications.com

Printed in Canada

Distributed in Israel by:
Shanky's
Petach Tikva 16
Jerusalem
972-2-538-6936

Distributed in Europe by:
Lehmanns
Unit E Viking Industrial Park
Rolling Mill Road,
Jarrow , Tyne & Wear NE32 3DP
44-191-430-0333

Distributed in Australia by:
Gold's Book and Gift Company
3- 13 William Street
Balaclava 3183
613-9527-8775

Distributed in South Africa by:
Kollel Bookshop
Northfield Centre
17 Northfield Avenue
Glenhazel 2192
27-11-440-6679

To Abba and Mommy,
With thanks for everything you've done for me.
May you have much nachas.

Chapter 1

"Bye!" Tehilla called over her shoulder as she pulled the front door closed behind her. She grinned as the door to the green minivan slowly rolled open, allowing her to climb into the car with her dignity intact. This was so much better than Mr. Stepanov's old, beat-up station wagon! She grimaced, remembering how she used to cram into the car with the other girls in her carpool. Things were definitely looking up for her. Not only was she traveling to school in style — if you could call a minivan "style" — but things there were about to get exciting. Very exciting.

"Good morning, Tehilla," came Sara Leah's voice from the back row. Predictably, she was hunched over a notebook with Adina.

"Morning, Tehilla," Shevy said brightly, still brushing her auburn hair into a ponytail. Tehilla stifled a laugh. Shevy tended to run late in the mornings and used the time spent traveling to school to get herself ready.

"Good morning," Penina chimed in. She was seated beside Sara Leah in the back.

"Morning," Tehilla replied, buckling herself into the seat beside Shevy. She leaned back and closed her eyes, as she usually did in the morning. She was not a morning person, and she preferred to spend the ride to school dozing off and relaxing. Today, though, sleep didn't come so easily.

"What time are choir tryouts?" Sara Leah suddenly asked, interrupting her study session with Adina.

Tehilla smiled and opened her eyes, the familiar feeling of nervous anticipation filling her. "They start during recess," she said. "And they continue until lunch. Miss Brickstein will call out girls to audition one at a time." She felt smug and confident. She, a seventh grader, was more informed than Adina and Sara Leah, the two eighth graders in the back seat.

"You're so lucky," Shevy said enviously. "I wish I knew how to sing. Imagine all the class time I'd get to miss for rehearsals!"

"Trust you to think like that," Adina chided.

"I couldn't wait to be in junior high," Shevy said, ignoring her sister. "I thought whoever wanted could be part of the choir. But then I found out…"

"…that only the girls with the best voices get to join," Penina interjected. "Lucky you, Tehilla, that you have such a good voice."

"Yeah," Shevy said enviously. "You get to miss so much class."

"That's not what I meant," Penina retorted. "Tehilla is lucky that she knows how to sing. It's such a beautiful gift."

Tehilla tossed her dark red ponytail in her self-assured manner. "We all have our talents, don't we?" she said magnanimously. But inwardly she was pleased with herself. Her clear, lilting voice that landed her solos in every performance fit very well with her image as the cherished only daughter of the Markson family. With two older brothers who were usually away at yeshivah, Tehilla relished her role as family princess.

The van glided to a stop right before it was supposed to merge onto the highway.

"Oh, no," Adina murmured, just as Shevy hopefully said, "Are we stuck in traffic?"

Tehilla laughed. "It's so funny that you two are sisters."

Adina flicked her notebook. "I hope we're *not* stuck in traffic," she said tightly. "I have a test first period today."

Sara Leah scanned the road in front of them. "Looks like it was just a red light," she said. "Nothing to worry about."

Adina breathed a sigh of relief as Shevy rummaged through her knapsack.

"May as well put my time to good use," Shevy said to herself.

"Shevy, you want to review for today's *Chumash* test?" Penina offered.

"Who, me?" Shevy asked, taken aback. "Nah, I'm gonna work on these." She held up a bag filled with small, colorful rubber bands. "I want to make a few bracelets now."

"Don't you have enough rubber-band jewelry?" Adina asked. "You've made so many different things you probably have enough to open up a store."

"Hey, that's a good idea!" Shevy said. "I should sell them."

"I think everyone has enough of her own," Tehilla said, holding up her own colorful wrist.

"Hey, I like your watch!" Shevy said admiringly. "How'd you do that?"

"I didn't," Tehilla replied, looking at her pink-and-white watch. "My friend Meira made it for my birthday. She took off the band from an old watch and made a new one out of rubber bands. Isn't it neat?"

"Sure is," Shevy replied. "That's a really cute idea."

"Did you bring along your loom?" Tehilla asked her. "I'll show you a new pattern I came up with."

Shevy shook her head. "I like to make these with my hands," she said. "It's easier that way."

"It's also easier for you to hide it from the teachers," Penina teased.

"Don't remind me," Shevy said mournfully. "I don't think I'll ever make another bracelet in Mrs. Barnet's class again."

"Shevy!" Adina said, horrified. "I don't believe you were making bracelets in class."

"Actually, I made some necklaces, too," Shevy said with a shrug. She looped a white rubber band over her fingers and then added a black one.

Penina giggled. "Shevy's not the only one. Mrs. Barnet was so upset that she said she's going to write a letter to the rainbow loom company complaining how their product keeps disrupting her class."

The other girls laughed, then lapsed into silence. Tehilla looked out the window, watching the cars whiz by on the highway. Their small community lacked a Bais Yaakov, and the girls had no choice but to travel to school each day.

All too soon the minivan pulled up to Machon Malka Mirtza.

"We're on time today," Adina noted with relief.

The girls thanked Mr. Stepanov for driving them as they piled out of the car.

"Off to another day of school," Shevy sighed.

Tehilla smiled. Another day of school, it certainly was. But it also promised to be a wonderful day at school.

"So, how'd it go?" Sara Leah asked Tehilla as the girls settled into the van on the way back home.

"How did what go?" Tehilla said, trying to sound modest. Of course, she knew exactly what Sara Leah was referring to.

"Did you get into choir?" Shevy asked eagerly.

"Of course she did," Penina answered for Tehilla. "How could Tehilla *not* get into choir?"

"Miss Brickstein is only going to post the choir list tomorrow," Tehilla said, smiling.

"Well, there's no question that you're in," Shevy said loyally.

Tehilla smiled dreamily, remembering last year's performance with her starring solo. From the way Miss Brickstein had smiled at her during tryouts, she dared to hope that she'd once again be given a solo — maybe even a few — in this year's performance.

"This year the choir is going to be a little bigger than last year's," Tehilla said suddenly. She frowned slightly. It seemed more exclusive to be part of a smaller group.

"I heard about that," Adina piped up. "Tzivi Brickstein — she's Miss Brickstein's sister — is in my class. She said a bigger choir will look more impressive at the school's *melaveh malkah*."

Tehilla sat up excitedly. Already she could envision the spotlight's warm lights on her face as the music rose to a crescendo, and with it her voice. She could hear the applause in the audience, and the smug satisfaction of knowing her mother and grandmother were somewhere out there, relishing the moment.

"Lucky you," Shevy said. "I wish I could sing at the *melaveh malkah*. But if I did, I might send the mothers running out of the room!" She chortled, and held up a bracelet. "Like this one?" she asked no one in particular. "I made it during English."

"I thought you said your teacher already caught you making one," Adina said, sounding very much like their mother.

"She did," Shevy said. "But today she had a substitute."

The girls began to compare their various pieces of handiwork and discuss different methods of weaving together the rubber bands. Only Tehilla remained quiet, oblivious to the conversation flowing around her.

When the minivan pulled up to the Markson house Tehilla quickly gathered her things together. With a hurried goodbye to her friends and a thank you to their driver, she darted up the path leading to her large, two-story house. Her mother opened the door after a hurried knock.

"Hi, Ma!" Tehilla said eagerly. She followed her mother inside the house, babbling excitedly. "Today we had choir tryouts, and I heard that we're going to perform at a *melaveh malkah*, and we'll find out who got into choir tomorrow..." She took a deep breath as she headed inside the kitchen. She probably wasn't making too much sense.

Her mother smiled as she watched her only daughter. "That sounds exciting, Tehilla."

Tehilla grinned happily. "Yeah." She sat down at the

kitchen table, noticing that her mother had set it for three. "Abba's coming home early?" she asked in surprise.

She was used to eating a cozy supper alone with her mother. Rabbi Markson usually came home later at night, after a long afternoon of work in his travel agency. He spent mornings learning in the local *kollel*.

Mrs. Markson nodded. "Actually," she said, "Abba and I have something important to discuss with you."

Tehilla started. There was something strange about her mother's tone. There was an undercurrent of excitement to it, but she also sounded nervous.

"Is everything okay?" Tehilla asked anxiously.

"Of course," her mother said. She busied herself cutting up tomatoes and cucumbers for a salad.

Tehilla relaxed. If everything was fine, that must mean her mother had some good news to share. Suddenly, she realized what must be going on.

"Is Baruch getting engaged?" she asked excitedly.

"What?" Her mother whirled around. "Why would you think that?"

Tehilla shrugged sheepishly. Her brother was twenty-one, and she hadn't overhead any tell-tale conversations concerning any upcoming nuptials, but then again, as a *shadchan* her mother was always on the phone about some *shidduch* or another.

"So what's going on then?" Tehilla asked. It was so unlike her normally placid mother to be so secretive.

"Abba will be home soon, and then we'll tell you all about it," Mrs. Markson assured her.

Tehilla felt a growing sense of apprehension. Something was going on, and she had no idea what it was. How in the world was she going to wait until her father came home and she found out what her parents were hiding?

Chapter 2

*T*ehilla jumped as she heard the front door open and the familiar sound of her father's heavy stride heading toward the kitchen.

"Hello," Rabbi Markson said as he sat down at the table.

"Hello," Mrs. Markson returned his greeting. She set a bowl of potato soup in front of him.

"Hi," Tehilla said hopefully. Now she'd find out what her parents had to tell her.

Her mother set a bowl in front of Tehilla, then brought a third one to the table. Tehilla tapped her feet impatiently against the table leg.

"So..." she began.

Mrs. Markson shook her head slightly. "Not now," she said. "Let's eat the soup before it gets cold."

Tehilla stared at the lumpy beige masses in front of her and sighed. Her mother was a fantastic cook, and her soup was no exception, but she had no appetite right now. Her mind whirled with possibilities as she glanced from her father to her mother. Were they moving? Had her father been offered a new job? Maybe they'd won the lottery? She rejected that one quickly. Her parents never bought lottery tickets. So what was going on, then?

"Eat, Tehilla," her mother urged. "Your soup will get cold."

Tehilla sighed, but picked up her spoon. Her parents' bowls were almost empty, she noted with satisfaction. Maybe they'd clue her in when they finished their first course.

Tehilla was midway through her bowl when she saw her parents exchange a glance. Her father coughed slightly and wiped his mouth with a napkin. Mrs. Markson toyed with the spoon she'd put down moments before. Tehilla sat up straight and eyed her parents expectantly. This was probably the moment she'd been waiting for...

"Sometimes," her father said slowly, "an opportunity arises when we can show Hashem how grateful we are for what He's given us."

Tehilla looked at him, confused. He sounded like he was about to deliver one of the trademark *shiurim* that had earned him his reputation in their small community of New Rosedale.

Rabbi Markson paused, looking thoughtful. "And sometimes we have an opportunity to stretch ourselves, to reach past our comfort zone and extend a hand to others."

Tehilla stared at her father. What was he talking about?

Mrs. Markson took over. "What we're trying to tell you, Tehilla, is that after thinking the matter through for a long time, and discussing it with many different people, we've decided…" She faltered, looked across the table at her husband, and then fixed her gaze on Tehilla. "We've decided to take in a girl who needs a home right now."

Tehilla blinked. *We've decided to take in a girl?* Had she just heard right?

"Actually, Rabbi Shutz called us and asked us if we could do it," Mrs. Markson explained. "He knows the family very well, and he also knows us very well, and…well, this girl needs a place to stay for some time."

"How long?" Tehilla asked quickly.

"At least until the end of the school year, maybe even longer."

Tehilla gaped. Until the end of the school year? Or even longer than that? Were her parents serious?

"We've already spoken with the girl's parents," Rabbi Markson said, "and she's going to be coming here on Sunday."

"What?" Tehilla exclaimed, her voice shrill. She couldn't believe this was happening. How had her parents made such a huge decision without mentioning it to her in the first place? She felt hurt and betrayed and...worried. She was Tehilla Markson, precious only girl. Her older brothers doted on her; her mother was her closest confidant. What would life be like with a stranger in the house? It was not a pleasant thought.

"The idea might take some getting used to," Mrs. Markson said compassionately, "but really, Tehilla, I think the experience will be good for you. And I think you'll enjoy having a sister, even if it's only temporary."

Tehilla gaped at her mother, and a sob gurgled up her throat. "A sister?" she managed in a tight voice. "Ma..." She fell silent, not trusting herself to speak. *I don't want a sister*, she wanted to say. *I'm your only daughter, and I'm used to things the way they are. I don't want them to change.*

"Why don't we tell you some details about her?" Mrs. Markson asked gently. "Her name is Henny Hart. She's almost twelve, so she'll be in sixth grade."

Tehilla stared morosely at her mother. "It's a good thing Mr. Stepanov got that minivan," Mrs. Markson remarked. "I don't know if we could have squeezed Henny into his old station wagon."

"What?" Tehilla spluttered. "She's going to my school?"

"Of course," her mother said. "She's going to live with us for now."

"But...but it's the middle of the school year." *And I don't want this strange girl tagging along everywhere I go*, she added silently.

"That's all right," her father put in. "We've talked it over with your principal and her parents. Everything will work out."

Tehilla sat back in her seat, arms crossed. It didn't seem like she had so much say in the matter.

"It'll take some getting used to," her mother said compassionately. "But I'm sure you two will become friends."

Tehilla blanched. No, they wouldn't! Why would she, popular Tehilla Markson, hit it off with some pitiful character who had to live with strangers?

A series of memories flashed through her mind, their edges sharp and painful. She and her mother were browsing through clothing racks, admiring a dark green sweater that would perfectly complement Tehilla's red hair. She was sitting at the kitchen table with her mother, deciding which new recipes to try out for Yom Tov. She was taking a stroll with her mother on a pleasant spring evening, talking lightly about anything and everything.

But all those good times were coming to an end. Her life, as she knew it, was going to change big time. This strange girl was going to ruin *everything*.

Tears blurred Tehilla's eyes as she stood up suddenly.

"Excuse me," she mumbled, before she turned and fled the room.

It'll be okay. It'll be okay. Tehilla tossed and turned as she remembered her mother's words. Mrs. Markson and Tehilla had had a long conversation that night, but all the while Tehilla couldn't help thinking, *Will this be the last one we have together before this girl comes?*

"It'll be okay, Tehilla," her mother had said. "Abba and I thought long and hard before we decided to do this. Henny really needs a home. She won't be here forever...it's just temporary until she can go back to her family."

"Why can't she stay with her family?" Tehilla blurted out, curious despite herself.

Her mother sighed. "That's not for here and now."

There was a long silence.

"What if she doesn't like it here?" Tehilla finally said. "What if *we* don't like *her*? What if — "

Her mother held up her hand to stop the flow of questions.

"There are a lot of 'what ifs' here, Tehilla," she said. "And I don't have all the answers. But I think we should take it slowly, okay? Don't worry so much...everything will work out."

Everything will work out. Tehilla snorted into her pillow. Yeah, right. A girl named Henny was about to enter her house, her life, and share everything — including her parents. How, she wondered miserably, had her peaceful existence turned so topsy-turvy in the span of a few hours?

Chapter 3

"Good morning," Mrs. Markson greeted Tehilla as she entered the kitchen.

Tehilla yawned, still rubbing her eyes. She hadn't slept too much last night, and she was tired. Her mother eyed her anxiously. Tehilla mustered up a wan smile. "Good morning," she said. She looked up at the big wall clock and headed to the counter. "No time for breakfast," she said. "Mr. Stepanov will be here any minute."

She took a banana and quickly pulled her lunch — a roll filled with tuna and lettuce — out of the fridge. Sure enough, the minivan's familiar honk filled the air.

"Gotta go!" Tehilla said. She ran to the closet, grabbed her jacket and knapsack, and turned around. "Bye!" she called, then ran out the front door.

She sighed with relief as she climbed into the minivan. She had no interest in rehashing last night's upsetting news with her mother. She knew her mother was worried about her reaction to their discussion, but she was too upset to talk about it.

"Morning, Tehilla!" Shevy said cheerfully. The other girls in the carpool greeted her in lower tones.

"Morning," Tehilla practically growled.

"Something happen to your voice?" Shevy asked. "You sound hoarse."

Tehilla shook her head. "Why do you..." She looked up at Shevy, who was grinning while trying to look innocent. Silly her. Of course her friends realized something was wrong. Thankfully, no one else said anything to her.

Tehilla stared out the window, not really seeing the houses and cars pass by. Her mind kept replaying last night's discussion. Why, she wondered desperately, did her parents want to take in someone else's daughter? Weren't they happy with the one they already had? She sighed loudly, and Adina, sitting beside her, stirred.

"A penny for your thoughts," she said lightly.

Tehilla stiffened. *A penny...a Henny. Henny. Henny. The girl who is coming to invade my space and my life.* She turned her head pointedly, making it clear that she was in no mood for any discussion. She wasn't being so polite, and she knew it, but she didn't have the heart to talk to her friends. Not now.

"Hi, Tehilla!" Breindy called. Tehilla gave her a wan smile as she walked into the seventh-grade classroom. "All ready for today's math quiz?" Breindy asked as Tehilla settled into her seat.

Tehilla stared at her, horrified. "I forgot all about it!"

Breindy raised her eyebrows incredulously. "You forgot about it? That's so not like you, Tehilla."

Tehilla didn't answer. She rummaged through her knapsack and took out her math notebook. Today's quiz had totally slipped her mind after last night's conversation with her parents. She pressed her lips together firmly. *Thank you, Henny,* she thought grimly. *We haven't even met yet, and already you're messing things up for me.* She tried to banish those thoughts from her mind and cram in a few minutes of studying.

"...posting choir results later," Devoiry was saying loudly.

Tehilla looked up from her notes distractedly. She'd totally forgotten about the choir. She shook her head, as if to push any thoughts about choir to a remote part of her brain. She'd think about that later. Right now she had to study. The bell rang a few minutes later, and Tehilla sighed. Maybe she'd get a few minutes during recess to review.

"Good morning, girls," Mrs. Gelber said briskly as she walked into the classroom. Her students stood up and waited until she reached her desk before they sat down. "Take out your siddurim, please."

There was a knock at the door, and Mrs. Gelber opened it to find Miss Brickstein standing there. A thrill of excitement ran through Tehilla when she saw the choir head.

"May I speak to Tehilla Markson for a moment, please?"

Tehilla looked up expectantly, aware that her classmates were all turning to look at her curiously. She sat up straight and looked hopefully at her teacher. Mrs. Gelber nodded, and Tehilla headed toward the door. What did Miss Brickstein want that couldn't wait until she posted the list of choir members?

Miss Brickstein smiled warmly at Tehilla as she joined her in the hallway. Tehilla smiled back shyly. In addition to being head of choir, Miss Brickstein was also head of G.O., and the junior-high students admired the lively, young teacher.

"Hi, Tehilla," Miss Brickstein said, flashing her warm, trademark smile. "I see your class is about to *daven*, so I'll make this quick." Tehilla looked at her curiously. "I'm posting the list of choir members today...and, needless to say, you're on it." The teacher smiled, and Tehilla grinned nervously. What was coming next?

"Anyway, I'm sure you know that, like last year, we'll be performing at the *melaveh malkah* for mothers and grandmothers of our students. I've composed a special song about generations linking together, and I thought it would be nice to have one girl sing the entire song, with the choir harmonizing in the background."

She looked at Tehilla, and Tehilla looked at her expectantly.

"I want that girl to be you," Miss Brickstein finished simply.

Tehilla blinked, flustered. "I called you out of class because the song is a bit complicated, and I'd like to teach it to you during recess over the next few days...that is, if you're interested in this solo." Miss Brickstein cocked her head and eyed Tehilla.

Tehilla's eyes shone, and a smile lit up her face. "Of course!" she said happily. "For sure!"

Already she could imagine the heady sound of applause, the compliments and accolades aimed her way days — no, even weeks — after the performance. Tehilla Markson, star soloist, was going to wow everyone in the audience. And she couldn't wait.

"Great, Tehilla," Miss Brickstein said, sending another warm smile Tehilla's way. "See you in the G.O. office at the beginning of recess, okay?"

"Okay," Tehilla confirmed with a nod of her head. She'd have to study for the quiz during lunch, but right now she couldn't care less. Her ponytail swished through the air as she headed to her seat, smiling with satisfaction. She cast her eyes downward to avoid her friends' wondering gazes. Let them think Miss Brickstein was simply telling her that she'd gotten into choir. This was one piece of news that she was going to keep secret. Everyone would find out in due time about her solo. Soon everyone would know that Tehilla Markson was the school's rising star.

"Hey, Tehilla, I saw your name on the choir list," Shevy said excitedly.

"Are you surprised?" Penina said, jabbing Shevy in the ribs.

Tehilla blushed as she fastened her seat belt.

"Miss Brickstein only takes the finest voices," Adina said. "Only six girls from my class are in the choir — and one of them is Tzivi Brickstein."

Tehilla smiled. She wasn't going to share the news with her friends about the song she'd be singing by herself. There'd be time for that yet. She was going to keep it a surprise from her mother, too. She couldn't wait to see her mother's face at the *melaveh malkah* when she sang an entire song by herself!

"Hey, Tehilla," Shevy spoke up again, "my mother told me that a girl is going to be boarding at your house."

Tehilla's smile was instantly replaced by a grimace. "How'd she hear that?" she asked, her eyes narrowing.

Shevy didn't notice her change in mood. "My mother's cousin's sister-in-law is neighbors with her family," she said. "Or something like that. But anyway, your mother told my mother last night."

"That's so nice," Sara Leah said. "How long is she staying by you?"

"I don't know," Tehilla said tersely.

"Lucky you," Shevy spoke up. "It was so enjoyable when Kaila stayed by my house, remember? And this girl will be staying by you for much longer. Such fun!"

Tehilla made a noise that sounded somewhat like a sob and a snort. *Fun!* she thought. *Shevy Kappel and her ideas of fun!*

"What grade is she in?" Penina wanted to know.

"Sixth grade," Tehilla mumbled.

"Yippee!" Shevy shouted.

Mr. Stepanov stepped on the brakes, hard, and the van squealed as it lurched to a stop. "What happened?" he asked, turning around in alarm.

"Er...um...nothing," Shevy said apologetically. "Sorry."

"Shevy," Adina sighed, shaking her head.

"I said I was sorry," Shevy insisted. She turned her attention back to Tehilla. "She's going to our school, right? My mother said she is." Tehilla nodded. "So she'll be in our class," Shevy said, clapping her hands excitedly. She turned to Penina. "We've got to tell everyone that we're getting a new kid in our class. And we'll have to plan a welcoming party. Tehilla, when's she starting school?"

"Monday," Tehilla said darkly.

"Great," Shevy said, clapping her hands. "Penina, let's start planning."

Sara Leah looked at her doubtfully. "I don't know about that," she said. "Maybe she'll be really shy and not want a party. Maybe she'll be really overwhelmed. I mean, it's so hard to start at a new school in the middle of the year. I think if you're just polite and friendly to her that should be enough."

Tehilla clamped her lips together disapprovingly. A welcoming party? Shevy wanted to throw a party to welcome this strange girl to their school?

Why, she wondered, would anyone care to welcome Henny Hart at all?

Chapter 4

Y ou look wonderful, Tehilla," Mrs. Markson assured her daughter. Tehilla had been standing in front of the hall mirror for half an hour already, smoothing her dark red hair and making sure her headband was perfectly in place. Tehilla smiled thinly and continued to pat her hair. Impressions, impressions. She had to make the best possible impression on the girl who'd be staying at her house.

"Ready?" Mrs. Markson asked, her gaze meeting Tehilla's in the mirror. Tehilla grimaced. "C'mon, Tehilla, it won't be so bad," Mrs. Markson said. "Give Henny a chance — you might like her." Tehilla sighed.

"Please, Tehilla, just be nice to her."

"I will be!" Tehilla was indignant. She might not like this Henny character, and she might not want her in her home, but nice she would be. No one could say that Tehilla Markson didn't know how to behave toward guests. "Why is she coming, anyway? Why can't she stay with her own family?" Tehilla asked, turning around to face her mother.

Mrs. Markson looked at Tehilla. "Extenuating circumstances, Tehilla. Maybe Henny herself will let you know when she's ready."

Tehilla scowled. Her mother was so into protecting other people's privacy. If this girl was coming to live with them, wasn't she entitled to know *why*?

"I know you'd like to know more about her," Mrs. Markson said. "But I'd rather wait for Henny to fill you in, if she'd like to. But I can tell you that she has three younger sisters, who'll be staying with her aunt."

"Why can't she stay with them?"

"Her aunt doesn't have room for one more. Besides, her own children are younger, too, and everyone thought it would be better for Henny to be with a girl closer to her own age."

Tehilla's scowl deepened. *Everyone thought so, didn't they? Make that everyone except for me.*

"There were no other aunts or uncles she could go to?" Tehilla asked.

"I suppose not. Maybe they can't take her in for whatever reasons. Look, Tehilla, we have lots of extra room, and our house is quiet. It'll be a big *chessed* for us to have her stay here."

Tehilla faltered for a moment, her heart going out to this unknown girl who had nowhere to go. Then she stiffened. She might feel bad for this Henny, but she didn't have to like her. Despite everything, Henny *was* going to be infringing on her privacy. She was just grateful she didn't have to share a room with her. That would have been intolerable.

Mrs. Markson looked at her watch. "She should be here any minute," she said.

Tehilla stifled the urge to go and call Meira to vent a little. No, she'd be on hand to greet this girl whenever she showed up. She mustered a polite smile to her face, ready to greet Henny.

The doorbell's clear chimes sounded through the large house.

"That must be her," Mrs. Markson said brightly. She went to open the door.

Tehilla hung back, folding her arms tightly.

"Hello," Mrs. Markson said warmly to a small group standing on the steps. "Come in, come in."

She ushered in a tall woman, her *sheitel* cut in a stylish bob. Beside her was a bearded man holding a toddler in one hand and a large suitcase in the other. Behind them trailed a petite girl, light brown hair pulled back tightly and accentuating her high cheekbones. Brown eyes flickered toward Tehilla, then looked away.

"This must be Henny," Mrs. Markson gushed.

Tehilla blanched.

"I'm Nechie Einhorn, Tehilla's aunt," the tall lady introduced herself. She pushed the bangs of her *sheitel* out of her eyes. "This is my husband and this" — she smiled fondly at the little boy — "is Shloimy."

"Thank you for driving Henny here," Mrs. Markson said. "I know it's a long trip."

"Oh, it was the least we could do," Nechie said. "You're doing so much for my poor sister...we're all so grateful."

Tehilla eyed the Einhorns with interest. They seemed young and nice.

"Would you like to stay for lunch?" Mrs. Markson asked.

Tehilla looked at them hopefully. Maybe, over the course of the meal, she'd find out why Henny was staying at their house.

"Oh, that's so kind of you," Aunt Nechie said. "But we have to get back. Sunday traffic is awful in the afternoon, and I left my two older children playing at friends' houses."

Tehilla exhaled, disappointed. Oh, well. So it would be just her, her mother, and Henny for the meal. That probably wouldn't go over so well.

"Take care, Henny," Aunt Nechie said, giving her niece a hug. "We'll be in touch, okay? Call me whenever you want to talk."

Henny smiled wanly at her. "Thanks," she said in a small voice.

Mrs. Markson and Tehilla exchanged a quick glance.

"Tehilla," Mrs. Markson said, "maybe Henny would like to see her room. Can you bring her upstairs?" Tehilla nodded. "My husband will bring up your suitcase when he gets home," Mrs. Markson told Henny.

"Okay," Henny said as she followed Tehilla up the stairs.

Tehilla swallowed hard as she tread on the familiar light pink carpeting. This was so, so strange. Here she was, leading a virtual stranger through the house she'd grown up in. Everything here was part and parcel of her very being, and now she was about to share it all with this girl. She was not happy about it, to say the least.

"Here you go," Tehilla said, trying to sound friendly. She groaned inwardly. She sounded more like a patient nervously awaiting a root canal. She hoped Henny didn't pick up on her less-than-happy attitude toward her.

"My mother spent hours picking out the linens and everything," Tehilla said. That was definitely true. She failed to mention how she, Tehilla, had refused to give any input on the room's décor.

The phone rang.

"I'm just going to take that call, okay?" Tehilla said quickly. It was probably one of her many friends, anxious to hear what the new girl was like. She dashed out of the room without waiting for a response.

"Hello," Tehilla said breathlessly into the extension in her room.

"Tehilla," came a familiar voice.

"Savta! How are you?"

Savta's chuckle came through the phone loud and clear. "*Baruch Hashem*, Tehilla. What's going on at your end?"

"Um...nothing much." Tehilla's voice dropped a few notches, and her shrewd grandmother heard it right away.

"What's wrong?"

"Nothing...just...Savta, you heard about the girl who's staying at my house?"

"I did, Tehilla, and I'm very impressed with your parents — and with you."

Tehilla didn't know if she should laugh or cry. "But Savta..." Tehilla paused. She quickly went to close the door to her room so Henny couldn't overhear her. "I didn't want her to come," she said in a hushed voice, just to be on the safe side. She waited nervously for Savta's response. Was her grandmother disappointed with her? "Savta, are you still there?" Tehilla ventured.

"I am, Tehilla." Her grandmother's voice sounded strong and assuring as usual, and Tehilla felt better. So Savta wasn't upset at her after all. "You're a normal girl, Tehilla. You've been the only child around the house for so long, and you're worried how things will be with someone else on your turf. It's overwhelming, I know."

"That's right," Tehilla said, filled with relief that someone understood her. "It's so...weird, and I don't even know why she's coming in the first place, and..."

"Your mother doesn't feel comfortable telling you about this girl's personal life," Savta interjected. "Your mother is always careful to respect other people's privacy."

Tehilla knew that, and though she admired that in her mother, it was causing her an awful lot of inconvenience right now.

"It doesn't really matter why she's staying with you," Savta continued. "Whatever it is, focus on the chance you have now to reach out to her, to make her feel welcome and accepted. Think about it, Tehilla. You have an ongoing chance to do *chessed* with this girl while she's at your house. Help her...smile at her...encourage her..."

Tehilla was silent. She hadn't thought about it like that, and she squirmed, embarrassed. She'd been so focused on herself that she hadn't thought too much about Henny.

"You hear me, Tehilla?"

"I do," Tehilla said slowly. "Yeah, I do. Thanks."

Savta laughed. "I'm proud of you, Tehilla. I know you can do it."

Tehilla squirmed. *I hope I can. All I know right now is... this won't be easy.*

"Anyway, Tehilla, just let your mother know that I'm taking her up on her invitation for Shabbos."

"You're coming this week?" Tehilla squealed. She didn't get to see her grandmother too often.

"That's right," Savta said. "I can't wait to see you."

"Same here!"

Tehilla hung up the phone, her face flushed. She'd better go see what her mother and Henny were — *Henny!* She'd completely forgotten about her guest! Who knew how long Henny had been waiting in her room?

Tehilla ran down the hall. The door to Henny's room was open, and there was no sign of her inside. She was probably downstairs. Tehilla bounded down the slightly winding staircase and into the kitchen. Sure enough, there was Henny sitting beside her mother. Her stomach twisted at the sight, and she faltered. Following through on Savta's advice was going to be hard — very hard.

"Sorry," Tehilla blurted out. "I lost track of time and..." She fell silent, feeling foolish. That didn't sound like too good an excuse. "Ma," she said quickly, trying to pretend that everything was fine, "that was Savta on the phone. She's coming for Shabbos."

"Great," Mrs. Markson said. "I'm sure she'll be thrilled to meet Henny."

Tehilla felt deflated. She'd forgotten that she wouldn't be having her grandmother to herself. Knowing Savta, she'd invest all her efforts into talking to Henny and getting to know her. She sighed. She just hoped she'd be able to follow at least some of Savta's advice.

"So, are you excited about starting school tomorrow?" she asked, trying to sound friendly.

"Not really," Henny answered candidly. "I mean, who likes school?"

Mrs. Markson laughed. "You might just like Machon Malka Mirtza. They do a lot of exciting things there."

Henny wrinkled her nose. "I'm sure it won't be like my old school. Every day there was a bundle of fun."

"I thought you said you don't like school," Tehilla said despite herself.

"Well, I don't like tests and boring classes and math and science," Henny explained.

Tehilla sat down at the table. She'd expected Henny to be shy, for some reason. It just fit with the image of a girl separated from her family for who-knows-what reason.

"Oh," she said, trying to think of something else to talk about. She mentally kicked herself. Popular Tehilla Markson always had something to say — except when it came to the strange girl who'd be sharing her life for the next few months.

Mrs. Markson got up from the table to prepare a light lunch.

"I'll help," Henny offered, standing up quickly.

Tehilla remained sitting at the table, feeling as if Henny had just ousted her from her position. *She* was the one supposed to be helping her mother.

It's a chessed, *Tehilla*, she heard her grandmother saying. *Help her...smile at her...encourage her...*

I can't do this, Savta, she wanted to wail. *Look at her... she doesn't need my help or encouragement. She's a perfectly fine, capable girl...and I want her to go home!*

"You arranged the vegetables so attractively," Mrs. Markson complimented Henny.

"Yeah, everyone says I'm good with my hands," Henny said matter-of-factly.

Tehilla stood up quietly and slipped out of the kitchen. It wasn't like she was needed there anyway.

Chapter 5

"Good morning," Tehilla mumbled wearily as she walked into the kitchen.

"Good morning," came Henny's voice. She was sitting at the kitchen table, eating a bowl of cereal.

Tehilla looked around the kitchen. Mrs. Markson was nowhere in sight. "Where's my mother?"

"She said she had to go somewhere. She left you a note." Henny gestured toward the counter, where a neon-pink notepad lay.

Tehilla gritted her teeth. It irked her that Henny was so

in the know. She headed over to the counter and picked up the paper.

Good morning, Tehilla!

Mrs. Berg from down the block just called. She's going to the hospital, and she asked me to get her children out this morning. Sorry I missed you…

Have a great day!

Tehilla stormed around the kitchen, putting together her lunch and snack. Today of all days her mother had to be gone.

A honk sounded outside.

"That's our ride," Tehilla said, scurrying out of the kitchen. "We've got to go."

Henny dumped her bowl in the sink and followed Tehilla to the coat closet. "I can't believe you actually spend so much time traveling to school," she said as she pulled on her jacket. "My old school was five minutes away from my house."

"Uh-huh," Tehilla muttered as she hoisted her knapsack onto her back. "Just close the door behind you," she instructed Henny. "It'll lock automatically."

"Good morning," Tehilla's friends greeted her as she climbed into the minivan.

"G'morning," she mumbled.

"You must be Henny," Shevy said eagerly as Henny entered the car.

Henny busied herself with closing her seat belt before she

responded. "Yeah, that's me," she said, suddenly sounding uncomfortable.

"I'm Shevy Kappel," Shevy said, as if it were obvious. "You're going to be in my class." Henny mustered a smile. "And this," Shevy said, gesturing flamboyantly, "is Penina Steinberg. She's also in our class."

"Hi," Penina said.

Sara Leah and Adina piped in with their introductions as well. Henny looked overwhelmed, and Tehilla felt almost sorry for her.

"Where'd you get that uniform from?" Shevy wanted to know.

Henny looked taken aback. "My aunt brought me over to see the school last week, and we picked up some blouses and skirts then."

Tehilla frowned. No one had offered *her* the chance to meet Henny before she moved in.

"The uniform in my old school was really pretty," Henny said. "Not like...like *this*." She wrinkled her nose as she looked down at the dark, pleated skirt.

"So, where are you from?" Shevy asked curiously.

"Um...Brooklyn," Henny said. "Flatbush, actually."

"Ooh, a real in-towner," Shevy said. "Well, I hope you like it here. It's different, that's for sure."

"In a good way," Adina hastened to add.

"New Rosedale is a really nice place to live," Sara Leah put in. "Everyone's very friendly."

"And Machon Malka Mirtza is the best school," Shevy said enthusiastically. "They're always doing fun G.O. activities."

"That's not what makes a school great," Adina chided.

"In my old school…" Henny began.

Tehilla sighed and looked out the window. It seemed like Henny had regained her footing. She thought drearily of the long day of school facing her, and suddenly brightened. She'd forgotten all about choir practice. If there was one thing she was looking forward to, it was this *melaveh malkah* performance.

All thoughts of Henny temporarily forgotten, Tehilla continued to look out the window, her eyes sparkling. Maybe today wouldn't be such a terrible day after all.

"Okay, Tehilla," Miss Brickstein said. "Let's get down to business."

Tehilla faced the choir head in the small G.O. office. From behind the closed door, the sounds of recess swirled about them, sounding as if they were from another world. Tehilla relished the feeling of being cut off from it all, focused on learning her solo.

"Did you have a chance to memorize the first few stanzas?" Miss Brickstein asked.

"I tried," Tehilla said with a shrug.

"You can still use the paper I gave you," Miss Brickstein

said encouragingly.

Tehilla nodded and glanced down at the dog-eared paper in her hand. She was pretty confident she knew the words, or almost all of them. When Miss Brickstein nodded her head, she began to sing. Her voice soared as she reached the chorus.

Links in a chain,
We're bonded together.
Sharing a legacy,
That will last forever.

Day follows day,
Year trails after year.
We'll always stay close,
We'll always be near.

"Great, Tehilla," Miss Brickstein said. "I'm going to be teaching the harmony to this song during tomorrow's choir practice, so I wanted to make sure you were getting the hang of it. Let's sing it a few more times, and then we'll practice again tomorrow during recess to make sure you've got it down pat."

Tehilla smiled and sang the song again, enjoying the sound of her voice as it filled the small room.

"Wonderful," Miss Brickstein said. "We'll meet again tomorrow, same time and place, okay?"

"Okay," Tehilla confirmed. She slipped out of the room,

feeling like she was walking on air. This solo — a whole song to herself — was a dream come true.

Tehilla hardly saw where she was going as she headed back to her classroom, enveloped in a hazy smugness. She was just rounding the corner when she passed the sixth-grade classroom. A group of girls was clustered outside of it. She could hear a familiar voice, loud and clear.

"Look at this bracelet," Shevy Kappel was saying. "My sister taught me how to make it. You need about a hundred rubber bands to do it!"

"Oh, that's nothing," came another voice. "In my old school, we made bracelets with maybe even two whole bags of rubber bands!"

Tehilla flinched. That could only be Henny, who was forever extolling the virtues of her old school. *If you liked it so much, Henny,* she wanted to say, *why didn't you just stay there?* Instead, she gritted her teeth and kept on walking. Only moments before she'd been floating. Somehow, seeing Henny Hart had made her tumble right back down to firm ground. And it wasn't a good feeling.

Chapter 6

"How's choir practice going, Tehilla?" Sara Leah asked from the back seat of the minivan.

"Fine," Tehilla said with a shrug. Actually, it was more than fine, especially when it came to her solo, but she was keeping that part under wraps for now.

"The *melaveh malkah* is pretty soon, isn't it?" Adina asked.

"Yeah, it's in another few weeks," Tehilla said, perking up.

"What choir are you talking about?" Henny wanted to know.

"The junior high has a choir every year," Penina explained. "There's going to be a *melaveh malkah* for mothers and grandmothers, and the choir performs at it."

"It's really fancy," Shevy put in. "I mean, I was never there... Only the girls in choir get to go, but I heard all about it from my mother. The choir puts on the same performance at a school assembly, too, after the *melaveh malkah* is over."

Tehilla smiled to herself. Yes, the *melaveh malkah* was a special occasion, and it was always fun to perform in front of her friends, too. Especially this year. She imagined the catcalls of "Tehilla" when she'd finish singing her song. She really couldn't wait.

"In my old school, we had a choir that performed every Rosh Chodesh," Henny said. "And every year we made a concert...the whole world came to it! We put on three per-formances, and each of them was sold out."

Tehilla stiffened. Trust Henny to outdo Machon Malka Mirtza with descriptions of her former school.

"Tehilla here has an amazing voice," Shevy gushed. "She's for sure going to get a huge solo."

Henny tossed her head, and her ponytail swished against Tehilla's cheek. "I always had at least three solos in my school's choir," she said proudly.

Tehilla eyed the girl sitting beside her. Must she always try to outdo everyone else?

"Did you remember to bring home your *Chumash*

notebook, Shevy?" Penina asked. "We have a test tomorrow."

"Um...let me check..." Shevy bent over her knapsack and started to riffle through it.

"I don't have to take any tests yet," Henny said smugly. "Anyway, I learned all this stuff two years ago — maybe even more. Your school is so behind."

Tehilla bristled. Surprisingly, no one else seemed to mind that comment.

"Could be," Adina said blandly. "But I think every school follows its own curriculum. If we're behind in one subject we're probably ahead in another."

Henny was about to reply when the minivan came to an abrupt stop.

"What's going on?" she asked.

"Looks like traffic," Sara Leah reported. "The highway can get pretty crowded on the way home."

"It's crazy to travel to school for so long," Henny remarked.

"Not everyone can live five minutes away from her school," Tehilla said tightly. She was grateful when Sara Leah began discussing something funny her younger sister had said.

"*My* little sisters are the cutest kids in the world, and I'm not exaggerating," Henny put in.

"You must really miss them," Sara Leah said softly.

An awkward silence settled over the car. Tehilla sensed Henny stiffen beside her. She felt almost bad for her. It must have been terribly difficult for Henny to be separated from her family — and for such a long time.

It's a chessed, *Tehilla,* she could hear Savta say. *Smile at her...help her...*

Tehilla shook her head slightly in self-reproach. Why did she keep forgetting that Henny was not in her house by choice?

"Hi, Ma!" Tehilla called as she pushed the front door open.

"Hi," her mother called back. She appeared in the hallway, a phone cradled between her head and shoulder.

"An excellent girl," she was saying. "Such a nice, refined family...and this girl's *middos* are something else."

Tehilla was used to her mother's long, *shidduch*-related phone conversations. Henny, though, stared at her wonderingly.

"My mother's a *shadchan*," Tehilla explained.

Henny's expression cleared. "My uncle is also a *shadchan*," she said. "I think he made over three hundred *shidduchim!* His phones — and he's got four of them, not including his cell phone — never stop ringing."

Tehilla didn't answer. She headed upstairs to get a head start on her homework before supper. Henny followed her up the stairs and disappeared into her own room.

"Supper, girls!" Mrs. Markson called about fifteen minutes later.

Tehilla clambered down the stairs. "It smells good in here!" she said, entering the kitchen.

Mrs. Markson pointed to the counter, where trays of brownies were cooling. "I figured I'd start baking for the Bergs' *shalom zachor*," she said, smiling.

"Oh, mazel tov!" Tehilla said. "That's so nice."

"Yes, it is," Mrs. Markson agreed. "Especially coming after five girls. Do you think you can babysit there tomorrow after school for an hour or two until their father gets home? I'll send over supper, and you can eat there with them."

Tehilla thought quickly. She didn't have any tests that week, and she hoped she wouldn't have too much home-work the next night. "Okay," she agreed.

"Great," Mrs. Markson said. "Maybe Henny will want to go along, too."

Tehilla looked up sharply. She was about to respond when Henny walked into the kitchen. "I'm all done with my homework," she said. "It was so easy. My homework in my old school used to take *hours*."

Mrs. Markson smiled. "How was your first day at Machon Malka Mirtza, Henny?"

Henny shrugged. "It was okay, I guess. The class is much smaller than what I'm used to, and the teachers were nothing like my old teachers..."

Tehilla turned away. If she had to listen to any more comparisons to Henny's "old school"...

"It must be so hard for you to start over in the middle of

the year," Mrs. Markson sympathized.

Henny shrugged again but didn't answer.

"Tehilla is going to babysit tomorrow night at a family down the block," Mrs. Markson said, changing the subject. "I thought you might want to go along and help her."

Tehilla stared at her mother, aghast. Since when had she agreed that Henny could tag along with her to the Bergs'?

"Okay," Henny said. "I've got lots of experience babysitting. All of my neighbors used to ask me to babysit."

While Tehilla glowered at her, the phone rang.

"Hello?" Mrs. Markson said. "Oh! How are you? Yes...? How's it going? I hear... She's settling in wonderfully... A real delight... No, thank *you* for letting us have her..." A few minutes later she handed the phone to Henny. "It's for you!" she said. "It's your mother."

Tehilla watched Henny's eyes light up as she took the phone. Suddenly she imagined herself, forced to stay at the home of strangers, far from anyone she knew and loved. She felt bad for Henny, she really did.

So why was it so hard for her to put up with this girl?

Chapter 7

*T*ehilla!" Sarala Berg squealed as she threw open the door.

Behind her trailed a woman wearing a short brown *sheitel*. She was already dressed in her coat and carrying a large handbag. "Hi," she said. "I'm Mrs. Berg's mother. Thank you so much for coming... I want to go see her in the hospital before visiting hours are over."

"No problem," Tehilla replied.

"The kids are in the living room," their grandmother said. "Bye, girls!" she threw over her shoulder. She hurried out the door, and Tehilla locked it behind her.

Sarala's eyes widened when she caught sight of Henny. "Who's that?" she wanted to know.

"It's my..." Tehilla trailed off uncomfortably. She couldn't exactly call Henny a friend, but it sounded strange to refer to her as a boarder.

Luckily, Sarala didn't seem to notice.

"Come see my new doll!" she insisted, pulling Tehilla into the room. She ran toward a pink toy stroller while Tehilla glanced around the living room. The five Berg girls, ranging in age from eight to two, were sprawled around the room. The six-year-old twins, Bashie and Yaffa, were busy trading stickers, the contents of their albums spilled all over the floor. The younger kids were hard at work, building a tower with what looked like every toy in the house. It was clearly a home where the mother was absent.

"What a gorgeous doll!" Tehilla said as Sarala thrust a small plastic figure in her direction.

"Tila!" little Shaindy lisped. Tehilla tousled her light blond curls.

"I hear you have a new brother!" Tehilla said.

"Brudder! Brudder!" Shaindy repeated happily.

"Come, everyone, to the kitchen. My mother sent over a yummy supper." Tehilla showed them the huge shopping bag she was carrying.

"What's inside?" Bashie wanted to know.

"Chicken and potatoes," Tehilla answered.

Yaffa scowled. "I don't like chicken."

"And I don't like potatoes," Simi chimed in.

"Well, I'm sure you'll like this," Tehilla said, trying to sound upbeat.

"No, I won't!" Simi insisted. "I never eat anything with potatoes. And I only eat my mommy's food."

"You don't have to eat potatoes if you don't want," Henny cut in smoothly.

Simi eyed her suspiciously. "Who are you?"

"I'm Henny. I'm staying at the Marksons' house."

"Why?" Yaffa demanded.

Henny flushed, and Tehilla bit her lip. She would have liked to know the same thing, but she felt bad for Henny.

"Who likes potato chips?" Tehilla said brightly, changing the subject. "My mother sent some along for whoever eats supper nicely."

"Yay!" The girls ran to the kitchen and seated themselves around the table.

"Er...Sarala, is the tablecloth *fleishig*?" Tehilla asked.

"Yeah," Sarala said. "And my *abba* said we should use plastic tonight. He left everything out on the counter." She pointed to a pile of plates, cups, napkins, and cutlery.

"Great," Tehilla said. "Who wants to help set the table?"

"I do!" Yaffa said.

"I want to set my own place," Bashie insisted.

"I don't let Yaffa touch my stuff!" Simi said loudly.

"Um...you know...maybe I'll do it myself," Tehilla said. She was surprised but gratified when Henny helped her.

That done, Tehilla placed the hot containers filled with chicken, potatoes, and salad on the table.

"I want salad!" Sarala announced. She pulled the container toward her.

"No!" Bashie shouted. "She's going to take the whole thing!"

"Am not," Sarala shot back. "And I'm allowed to take by myself."

"I don't like tomatoes," Simi declared.

"So no tomatoes or potatoes for you, then," Tehilla said lightly.

"No chicken for me!" Yaffa shrieked as Tehilla uncovered the container. Tehilla looked at her uncertainly. Mrs. Markson always made sure Tehilla ate some protein.

"It's okay," Henny spoke up. "You don't have to eat it."

Tehilla looked at her dourly. Since when was Henny in charge here? She decided not to make an issue of it, though. Nothing would happen to Yaffa if she missed eating protein at one meal.

"You coughed on my food!" Yaffa suddenly shrieked. She shot daggers at Bashie, who was shaking her head adamantly.

"I did not!"

"Did too!"

"I won't eat my food now," Yaffa said, pouting. She pushed her plate away.

Tehilla wasn't sure what to do. Should she insist that Yaffa eat her food?

"Where's the ketchup?" Henny said suddenly.

"I'm taking ketchup first," Sarala said, dashing to get it. She returned to the table a moment later.

Henny reached out her hand for the ketchup bottle. "Who wants a smiley face on her food?"

The girls looked at her. "Me!" they all shouted.

Henny patiently drew red smiley faces on everyone's plates. Even Yaffa decided to eat her food after it was duly decorated.

Tehilla looked on, impressed despite herself. Supper was over only fifteen minutes after it began.

"Okay, pajama time now," Tehilla said.

"Mommy lets me put on pajamas late," Sarala said.

Tehilla looked at her doubtfully. Mrs. Markson had specifically told her to make sure the kids were in pajamas before their father came home.

"I don't like pajamas!" Yaffa shouted.

"I want my mommy to put them on!" Simi shrieked.

"Mommy! Mommy!" Shaindy called.

Oh, no. Tehilla eyed the mutinous girls nervously. There were going to be a few full-fledged tantrums here if she didn't take control of the situation fast.

"Whoever puts on pajamas nicely gets potato chips after," Henny spoke up.

There were a few half-hearted protests, but the promise of a treat was enough to spur the girls up the stairs and into their bedrooms.

Why didn't I think of that? Tehilla wondered.

In no time, the girls were ready for bed. They chomped happily on their potato chips.

"Teeth brushing time!" Tehilla announced when they were done.

"I don't like to brush teeth!" Yaffa declared.

"I want my mommy to do it!" Simi said.

"Who wants to hear a funny story?" Henny spoke up. "I'll tell it to you right after your teeth are brushed."

Tehilla watched as the girls followed Henny to the bathroom, feeling like a third wheel. There was no denying that Henny had a knack with kids.

A knock sounded on the front door, and Mr. Berg came in while Henny was in the middle of her story.

"Not yet, Daddy!" Sarala said. "We want to hear the end of the story."

"Please, Henny, can you stay just a few more minutes?" Yaffa begged.

"How about if I come back a different day?" Henny asked, extricating herself from the tangle of girls.

The Berg children pouted.

"Thank you so much," Mr. Berg said to Henny and Tehilla as they headed out the door.

"You're welcome," Tehilla said politely. If only he knew who'd really been running the show tonight...

The girls were quiet as they walked home together.

"You're good with kids," Tehilla commented reluctantly.

She meant it more as a statement than a compliment.

"I have three younger sisters," Henny said matter-of-factly. "And I had to help out a lot at home, so I guess I learned on the job."

She sounded wistful, and Tehilla wondered if she was thinking of her little sisters. Henny hardly spoke about them — or about her parents either, for that matter.

The girls were silent as they turned up the walk leading to the sprawling Markson house.

"Hi, girls!" Mrs. Markson greeted them. "How'd it go tonight?" Without waiting for an answer, she turned to Tehilla. "I'm on the phone with Savta," she said, gesturing to the phone cradled between her head and shoulder. "She wants to speak to you."

Tehilla eagerly took the phone from her mother. "Hi, Savta."

"Hello to you, Tehilla. How are things going?"

Tehilla paused. "Well..." She thought of Henny, and how unnatural it felt to have her around the house. She thought of the way Henny was always comparing things to what she was used to, and how downright annoying that was. Then she recalled babysitting at the Bergs' just moments ago, and how Henny had seemed so competent and reliable. It was all just so confusing.

Savta seemed to understand everything Tehilla left unsaid. "Just remember, Tehilla," she said. "You're doing an incredible *chessed*."

"I know," Tehilla sighed. "I know."

So why, she wondered when she hung up the phone, didn't she feel any better?

Chapter 8

Okay, girls," Miss Brickstein said, clapping her hands for attention. "Today we're learning a new song." The girls in her choir looked at her expectantly. "For this song," Miss Brickstein continued, "we're doing something different. Tehilla Markson is going to sing it solo, while the rest of you harmonize in the background."

Tehilla blushed, feeling all eyes upon her.

Devoiry Blum, standing beside her, elbowed her in the ribs. "Why didn't you tell us?" she whispered.

Tehilla shrugged. She'd wanted the news to come as a surprise to everyone, so she'd have more of a chance to shine. But of course, she couldn't share that with her friends.

"So here goes..." Miss Brickstein said. She handed out sheets with the words of the song and started to teach the harmony.

Tehilla listened, smiling to herself. The song was so beautiful; the audience was going to love it. And she was going to love singing it to them.

"Okay," their teacher said once the girls had sung the first stanzas repeatedly. "I think you girls have got the beginning of the song down pat. Tehilla?" She nodded at Tehilla, who stepped forward. "Let's try it out together now," Miss Brickstein said. "You sing, and we'll harmonize."

Tehilla cleared her throat nervously, then opened her mouth. As she sang, she listened to the choir blending with her voice in the background. She smiled, gaining confidence. They sounded great.

"Good job," Miss Brickstein said happily. "You girls sound amazing. I have to leave early today, so we'll end here. But girls!" she called after them as they turned to go. "You have homework tonight!" Some girls looked at her curiously; others groaned. "Please memorize the words of the song tonight," Miss Brickstein said. "Once we've finished learning this song we're going to move on to learning choreography."

"What's that?" asked a petite sixth grader.

"The motions," Miss Brickstein replied, waving her hands

for emphasis. "And we've got lots of them to learn before the big day! Bye, girls!" She sailed out of the room, leaving behind the girls in choir.

"Too bad choir practice ended early," Devoiry grumbled. "We won't get to miss so much class today."

Tehilla grinned. She sounded so much like Shevy.

"You sound amazing, Tehilla," gushed Faigie, an eighth grader.

"Yeah," said Yael, another eighth grader.

"Thanks," Tehilla replied, trying to sound modest.

She turned to leave the classroom. As she opened the door, Shira Levy, a sixth grader, appeared at her side.

"Tehilla," she said, "Henny Hart is staying at your house, right?"

Tehilla nodded, frowning slightly.

"Is it true that she lives in a mansion with two full-time maids?" Shira asked breathlessly.

Tehilla was taken aback. She had no idea what type of house Henny was coming from, but Henny didn't really fit the picture of a wealthy girl.

"Um..." She racked her brains, trying to think of something to say.

"And is it true that her parents are away on top-secret business in Europe?" Shira continued.

Tehilla's frown deepened. If they were, she certainly didn't know about it. But this whole conversation was more than a bit strange... "I've got to go," she told Shira abruptly. "I don't want to miss too much class." She hurried away, the questions buzzing in her head like noisy little bees.

"I heard you got a major solo!" Shevy crowed as she propelled herself into Mr. Stepanov's minivan. She sounded as excited as if she herself had landed the solo.

"Yeah," Tehilla replied. She'd relished thinking of the moment her big news would become public, but right now she couldn't even enjoy it. She was too busy mulling over Shira's unsettling questions earlier that day.

"Everyone's talking about it," Adina said.

"What's so major about a solo?" Henny said flippantly. "I used to get them all the time."

I'm sure you did, Tehilla thought, turning icy eyes on her. *Just like I'm sure your parents own a mansion, or that they're gallivanting around Europe. Or…are they?*

"Tehilla is going to sing an entire song by herself," Shevy said importantly.

"Last year I sang *two* whole songs by myself at my school's concert," Henny said proudly.

"Really now," Tehilla drawled, turning to Henny. "I can't imagine your teachers let one girl have two solos."

"But they did," Henny insisted. "It's because of my voice."

Tehilla eyed her in disdain. *I bet you can't carry a tune for the life of you*, she wanted to say.

Instead, she clamped her lips shut and stared unseeingly out the window. She couldn't wait to get home and tell her mother what type of girl they'd taken into their house. Tehilla tapped her foot impatiently as the trip home seemed to crawl by.

Finally, Mr. Stepanov pulled up in front of the Markson house. Tehilla said a quick "goodbye" to her friends and a "thank you" to Mr. Stepanov before running up the walk to her house.

"Ma?" she called as she unlocked the door and stepped inside. There was no answer. "Ma?" she tried again.

"Didn't your mother say she was going to a wedding and wouldn't be home?" Henny offered, coming in behind her.

Tehilla glowered at her, as if her mother's absence was Henny's fault. She'd totally forgotten that her parents were going to be gone for the night. Mrs. Markson had been the *shadchan* for tonight's *chassan* and *kallah*, and though she didn't attend every wedding she was invited to, she'd grown particularly close to this *kallah*.

The phone rang, and she lunged for it. It was Meira.

"Hi!" she said, eager to speak to someone — anyone — besides for Henny.

"I forgot my homework pad in school," Meira said. "Do you mind reading to me what you wrote down?"

"Sure," Tehilla said. "Just let me go upstairs first, okay? I just got home."

As she headed up the stairs she toyed with the idea of

confiding in Meira. She was convinced now that Henny was nothing more than a silly girl who liked to make up outlandish stories and get attention for them. It was disgusting, really. She checked that her bedroom door was firmly closed before turning her attention to the phone.

"Do you want to study over the phone later for the *Chumash* test?" Meira asked as she waited for Tehilla to open her homework pad.

Tehilla's mind flitted to what they'd learned that day in *Chumash*. The *meraglim*, scared of the giants they'd seen in Eretz Yisrael, spoke *lashon hara* about the Land. They were punished...and Bnei Yisrael were still suffering the ramifications of their misplaced words.

No, she wouldn't vent to Meira. She'd talk the matter over with her parents instead.

"Tehilla, are you still there?" Tehilla shook her head, as if trying to clear it, and turned her attention to Meira.

"Yeah, I am." She proceeded to give Meira the assignment and hung up the phone. A moment later it rang again.

"Tehilla?"

Tehilla almost jumped for joy. It was her mother. There was music in the background, and it was hard to make out Mrs. Markson's voice.

"Tehilla, I left supper warming in the oven for you and Henny, okay?" Mrs. Markson said.

"Okay, thanks. Ma?"

"What, Tehilla? Did you say something?"

"Ma, I wanted to ask you something."

There was a crackling noise, and then Mrs. Markson's voice faded in and out. "Sorry, Tehilla. I don't have good reception here." Tehilla sighed in frustration. "We'll be home late tonight, after you're sleeping."

Tehilla couldn't hear what else her mother had to say, because the call disconnected right then and there. She pushed the "off" button, hard, and sat down moodily on her bed.

This was so not fair. Tonight of all nights, her mother had to be away. And she had to eat supper alone with Henny — not to mention spend the whole night together under the same roof.

Tehilla thought about spending the night in her room, but then nixed the idea. She was hungry, and besides, her mother was depending on her to make sure Henny ate supper. She stomped out of her room and down the hall.

"Henny," she called. "I'm eating now. Do you want to eat now or later?"

"Later," Henny answered. Her voice sounded muffled, and Tehilla wondered if she was crying. Well, she told herself, even if she were, it served her right.

Tehilla turned around, her eyes hard, and flounced down the stairs. She helped herself to sweet-and-sour meatballs and brown rice, and sat down at the table. It was strange to eat by herself, she had to admit. Still, it would've been a lot more uncomfortable to eat alongside Henny.

Chapter 9

"Wake up! Wake up!"

Tehilla sat up in bed, disoriented and confused. The talking alarm clock her brothers had given her as a birthday gift was blaring full force. Tehilla glanced at the numbers on the clock and groaned. 6:45. She'd forgotten that she'd set the alarm to go off a full fifteen minutes early so she'd have time to talk to her mother that morning before she left for school.

She leaned back on her pillows and cuddled into her thick, warm blanket. A few extra minutes of sleep seemed so tempting, but she couldn't go a whole day without speaking to her mother about Henny and the stories she was telling her classmates.

Tehilla climbed out of bed and was downstairs in a record five minutes. Still smoothing down her hair, she walked into the kitchen. She smiled when she caught sight of her mother, sipping a cup of coffee. Her smile quickly turned to a deep frown, however, when her eyes fell on Henny, who was sitting beside her and eating a bowl of cereal.

"Good morning, Tehilla," her mother said. "You're up early today. You even have enough time to eat breakfast at home."

"Mm-hmm," Tehilla mumbled absently. "How was the wedding?" she asked, trying to figure out how to get her mother to herself.

"Oh, it was beautiful," her mother answered. "Really something special."

"Ma," Tehilla said, "can I talk to you for a minute?"

"Sure," Mrs. Markson said. She took one final sip and put down her mug. "What do you want to talk about?"

Tehilla shot pointed glances at Henny, who was calmly pouring herself another bowl of Cheerios.

"Um...not in here," she muttered.

Her mother looked surprised but followed her out of the room. Tehilla walked to a corner of the living room, near a large window, and faced her mother. "Look, Ma," she whispered, trying to make sure Henny couldn't overhear her, "we've got a problem." Mrs. Markson raised her eyebrows but waited for Tehilla to continue. "I think Henny is...well, I think she's telling the sixth grade made-up stories — like one girl asked me if she lives in a mansion. She also wanted to know if Henny's parents are in Europe. Ma, are they?"

Mrs. Markson was quiet for a moment. "Don't worry about it, Tehilla," she finally said. "Right now, all I ask is that you give Henny her space and just be nice to her."

"But Ma, are those things true?"

Mrs. Markson was opening her mouth to answer when Henny walked into the room.

"Oh, there you are!" she said. "Tehilla, you're going to be late." She looked pointedly at her watch.

Tehilla gritted her teeth in annoyance and looked helplessly at her mother. Her mother shook her head slightly. "Not now," she murmured, so Henny couldn't hear.

Tehilla sighed and went to the kitchen to get her lunch and snack.

"He's here!" Henny announced, looking out the kitchen window. Sure enough, a loud honk sounded.

"Have a good day," Mrs. Markson said brightly. She gave Tehilla a reassuring smile.

Tehilla headed out the door, more confused than ever before. Was Henny making up these stories or not? Her mother hadn't seemed too perturbed. Was it really possible that Henny was the daughter of a millionaire? What, then, was she doing at the Marksons' house? She groaned inwardly. This was all just so confusing.

Tehilla ambled down the hallway with Meira, sidestepping groups of girls enjoying their few minutes of recess.

"My sister decided on navy for her color scheme," Meira was saying. "My whole family looks best in that color. My mother is going to take us on Sunday to look for gowns."

"Lucky you," Tehilla said dreamily. She couldn't wait until her brothers got married and she, too, could wear a long, flowing gown.

They passed the sixth-grade classroom. A group of girls stood outside, talking excitedly and showing off their latest rubber-band creations. Shevy was there, and so was Penina. Tehilla wondered fleetingly where Henny was. She peeked inside the classroom and saw Henny sitting alone at her desk, looking forlorn. She suddenly realized that Shevy and Penina hadn't been speaking much to Henny during their trips to and from school. What was going on?

"Wait one second," Tehilla said to Meira. "I've got to speak to Shevy for a minute."

"Um, Shevy?" Tehilla said, tapping Shevy on the

shoulder. Shevy whirled around and brightened when she saw Tehilla.

"Tehilla Markson, star soloist of Machon Malka Mirtza!" she announced loudly. The sixth graders stopped their conversation and gazed admiringly at Tehilla. Tehilla flushed.

"Shevy, can I speak with you privately for a minute?"

"Of course!" Shevy said eagerly.

Tehilla wondered wryly if she should've spoken to Penina instead, but it was too late. She led Shevy a few feet away from her friends. "Listen, Shevy," Tehilla said in a hushed voice. "Is something going on with Henny?"

"What do you mean?" Shevy looked surprised.

"I don't know... It's just that she's sitting all alone during recess, and she looks kind of sad."

Tehilla wasn't sure why she was mixing in. After all, hadn't she been the one who was upset at Henny? Why was she now trying to improve Henny's social life?

Shevy looked uncomfortable. "She's fine, I think," she said, not sounding at all convincing.

"Do the girls like her?" Tehilla asked forcibly. She regretted the question the minute it was out of her mouth. "Never mind... I don't want to speak *lashon hara*." She bit her lip, not sure what to say next. "Forget it, Shevy. Thanks." She gave Shevy a small smile.

"Okay," Shevy said, shrugging. She bounded back to her friends while Tehilla rejoined Meira.

Meira lapsed back into a discussion about her sister's wedding preparations, but Tehilla's mind kept wandering. Seeing Henny looking so lonely tugged at her. True, she found Henny annoying, and it was hard to know if she was even telling the truth half the time, but who knew what was going on in Henny's private life? It couldn't be anything too good, that was for sure.

"One second, Meira," Tehilla said. "Do you mind if we turn around? I need to go back to the sixth grade for a minute." Meira, still absorbed in a detailed account of her sister's search for the perfect white shoes, nodded. "Wait for me a minute, okay?" Tehilla said as she walked inside the sixth-grade classroom.

Henny was staring out the window and didn't notice her approaching. "Hi, Henny," Tehilla said, trying to infuse some warmth into her voice.

Henny turned around. "Oh, hi," she said, looking surprised.

"Um…" Tehilla suddenly felt awkward. "I just wanted to see how you're doing."

"Oh! Thanks." Henny smiled, looking grateful.

"Okay, then," Tehilla said lightly. "I'd better get back to class before the bell rings. Bye."

"Bye," Henny replied.

Tehilla gave her a small wave and left the classroom.

"What're you doing here?" Penina asked as she left the room.

"Oh, nothing," Tehilla said, waving her hand dismissively.

"Everything's fine." She pasted a smile on her face, though inwardly she blanched. Everything was absolutely *not* fine. She'd have given anything to know why, exactly, Henny looked so miserable.

Chapter 10

I'm so relieved it's Erev Shabbos," Adina commented as Mr. Stepanov's minivan bore them away from Machon Malka Mirtza for the weekend.

"Me too," Sara Leah agreed. "It's been a long week."

Tehilla drummed her fingers on the seat in front of her. It seemed like Henny had been with their family for a lot longer than a week.

"My grandmother is coming for Shabbos," Tehilla spoke up.

"That's so nice!" Penina commented.

"Does that mean you're not coming to the assisted living

facility on Shabbos?" Sara Leah asked. "Mrs. Kanter will be so disappointed."

"Well, the rest of you will go visit her, won't you?" Tehilla asked.

"Still, she likes when all of us, the whole carpool clan, come," Sara Leah said. "But it's okay. Enjoy your grandmother."

"Carpool clan?" Henny said, raising her eyebrows.

"That's what our school secretary calls us, so other people started calling us that, too," Adina explained.

"And you go to the assisted living place every week?"

"We try," Adina replied. "Mrs. Kanter, one of the ladies there, is like an adopted grandmother to us. She actually ended up being related to a girl who stayed by our house for two weeks, but they didn't know that before they met."

Shevy was noticeably absent during this discussion. Tehilla looked over at her. There were bags of rubber bands on Shevy's lap, and she was busy looping the small colorful bands on her fingers.

"Why so many, Shevy?" Tehilla asked.

"Hmm?" Shevy said absently.

"Why are you making so many bracelets?"

"I'm making key chains," Shevy corrected her. "My class likes to make key chains out of rubber bands."

"It's kind of like a contest," Penina explained. "Everyone's trying to see who can make the most key chains."

"We weren't like that when *we* were in sixth grade," Adina

said condescendingly, sounding as if she were decades older than her sister.

"Oh, yeah?" Sara Leah challenged, laughing. "We had our own silly contests, don't you remember? Like, who could collect the biggest bag of eraser shavings? And who could collect the biggest clumps of dried glue?"

"Eew," Shevy said, scrunching up her nose. "That's weird."

Tehilla looked at Henny. She was very quiet, and she looked uncomfortable. Her own knapsack was noticeably free of key chains, save for a small smiley face dangling from one zipper. She'd barely been at the Marksons' for a week, and already she looked so unhappy. Tehilla suddenly wondered guiltily if she, perhaps, had a role in that...and if she could somehow change it.

"I heard that Miss Brickstein is giving out solos for choir next week," Shevy remarked.

"Are you trying out for one, Tehilla?" Penina asked.

Tehilla shook her head. "Miss Brickstein wants to limit solos to one per girl."

"And Tehilla's solo is like ten in one!" Shevy put in.

Tehilla flushed and waited for Henny to pipe up with one of her stories about being assigned who-knows-how-many solos. Henny merely sighed and looked listlessly out the window.

"I wish we could all go to the *melaveh malkah*," Penina said wistfully.

"Yeah," Shevy agreed loudly. "It's not fair that just the

choir girls get to go. *And* they get to miss so much class, too."

"You're obsessed with missing class, Shevy," Adina chided. "But I also wouldn't mind going to the *melaveh malkah*. My mother always says how beautiful it is."

"It is," Tehilla remarked. "It's really fancy, from the food down to the tablecloths."

"How many songs is the choir singing?" Sara Leah wanted to know.

"So far we've learned four songs, and I think we're still going to learn a few more."

Tehilla smiled as her friends continued to pepper her with questions. This was one event she was looking forward to — that was for sure. Soon enough the minivan rolled to a smooth stop in front of the Markson house. Henny quietly slid out of the car.

"Good Shabbos!" Tehilla called, waving to her friends. "Thank you," she said to Mr. Stepanov.

"*Gut Shabbos*," he said in turn, before driving off.

Tehilla practically danced up the walk to her house. Savta was surely there already; she'd said she'd be arriving in the morning.

"Hello," Tehilla called as she opened the door.

"Is that my Tehilla?" Savta asked, her tall frame entering the hallway. She looked poised and put-together as usual, her light blond *sheitel* styled to perfection and her navy suit giving no sign that she'd just traveled for two hours.

Everyone Savta met always marveled how she looked far younger than her age. Tehilla fell happily into her grandmother's arms.

"And you must be Henny," Savta said, bestowing her gracious smile on Henny.

Henny smiled tentatively, looking slightly awed. Tehilla watched her grandmother proudly. She certainly had a commanding presence. It wasn't for nothing that she'd spent thirty years as principal of a girls' high school.

"I've heard such nice things about you," Savta said. Henny flushed.

Tehilla eyed her strangely. It was so unlike Henny to be so quiet. She usually seemed much more sure of herself.

"I'm sure we'll become better acquainted over Shabbos," Savta said kindly. Tehilla flinched. She didn't get to see her grandmother too often; it didn't seem fair to have to share her now. Savta looked at Tehilla and gave an imperceptible wink. Tehilla smiled slightly, feeling better. Maybe things wouldn't be so bad after all. Savta retired to the guest room to rest, while Tehilla went to the kitchen to help her mother with Shabbos preparations.

"Can I do something?" Henny asked, trailing behind Tehilla.

Tehilla bit her lip. Somehow, Henny had once again beat her to it. Mrs. Markson looked up from the salad she was preparing. "Hi, girls," she said. "Thanks for the offer, but we're just about done here. Why don't you go upstairs and get ready for Shabbos?"

Henny looked surprised, but Tehilla was unfazed. Shabbos in the Markson home was ushered in calmly, without the usual frantic wave of preparations that took place in other households. Half an hour later Tehilla was downstairs again, showered and dressed in a new two-piece outfit.

"You look so nice," Mrs. Markson said.

"Thanks," Tehilla replied. They'd found the outfit at a store that was going out of business, and the merchandise had been slashed to half price.

"Ma," Tehilla said, "about Henny..."

"Yes?"

"Remember what we were talking about the other day?"

"I do, Tehilla, and all I can tell you is to try to put yourself in Henny's shoes." Mrs. Markson paused for a moment, looking reflective. "She's away from her family for months on end; she's staying with a strange family and forced to enter a new school in the middle of the year..."

"Why didn't she stay at her regular school?" Tehilla interjected. "Couldn't she live with one of her friends?"

Mrs. Markson shook her head. "Not many families can take in another child for such a long time. People have small houses and big families; people have other commitments... So just remember, Tehilla, that she's going through a hard time. Be patient with her. I know it's not easy."

Tehilla looked thoughtful. "But still..."

A slight rustle caught her attention, and she looked up to find Henny standing in the doorway of the kitchen. She was dressed in a long Shabbos robe, and she looked uncomfortable.

"Um…do you get dressed on Friday nights?" she asked awkwardly, eyeing Tehilla's outfit. "Should I change?"

"You can wear whatever you feel comfortable in," Mrs. Markson said assuringly. "Tehilla's outfit is new, so she wanted to wear it tonight." Tehilla looked at her mother. The Marksons didn't usually wear robes, but it was thoughtful of her mother to make Henny feel comfortable. "Your robe is really beautiful," Mrs. Markson said, looking it over. "Isn't it, Tehilla?"

Tehilla nodded quickly, taken aback. It was nice enough, but it wasn't anything that Tehilla — or her mother, for that matter — would have picked out from the store.

"Thank you," Henny said demurely. Her eyes clouded, and she looked wistful. "My mother and I bought it together last year."

There was silence for a moment. "I'm sure your mother has just as good taste as you do," Mrs. Markson said softly. She quickly changed the subject. "Girls, would you like some cake? It's a new recipe."

"Sure," Tehilla said. Henny nodded. "I'll serve it, Ma," Tehilla offered. "You can go get ready for Shabbos."

"Thanks, Tehilla," her mother replied, smiling at the girls. "I'm going to take a short nap."

When they could hear her footsteps on the stairs, Henny turned incredulously to Tehilla. "A *nap*? Your mother gets to nap on Erev Shabbos?"

"Yeah," Tehilla said matter-of-factly. "She's very organized and makes most of the food on Thursday. When I was little my family used to go on local trips on Erev Shabbos, when Shabbos started later."

"Wow," Henny said, shaking her head. "My house is so different. My mother does all her cooking on Friday morning."

Tehilla's eyes narrowed. Here, maybe, was her chance to find out if Henny was telling the truth. "Well, I guess it's not a big deal if she has so much help," she said nonchalantly.

"My little sisters are not much help," Henny said, reaching for a piece of marble cake that Tehilla had just cut. "And when I came home from school on Friday, there was still tons to do."

"You don't have cleaning help or maids?" Tehilla held her breath.

Henny shook her head. "My mother doesn't like having outside help in the house," she said. "When she was little my grandmother's cleaning lady stole all her jewelry, and since then my mother is afraid of taking in cleaning help."

"Really?" Tehilla said, trying to keep her voice even. "That's strange. Someone told me that she heard your mother has full-time help in the house...I mean, your mansion."

Henny stared at Tehilla, looking stricken. Tehilla gulped hard, realizing too late that she had gone too far. Why, oh, why, hadn't she just kept quiet? An awful silence hung over the kitchen, thick and foreboding. Suddenly, Henny pushed back her chair, bolting from the kitchen. As Tehilla listened to her footsteps pounding up the stairs, she glanced bleakly at Henny's half-eaten piece of cake. What, she wondered miserably, had she just done?

Chapter 11

So, Henny, how do you like it here in New Rosedale?" Savta looked disarmingly at Henny from her armchair.

"Um...it's okay," Henny replied. "I mean, I haven't really seen much of it, to be honest."

"Tehilla will take you around one day, I'm sure," Savta said.

Tehilla looked at her grandmother. Had Savta noticed that she and Henny hadn't exchanged a word that day — and not the day before either?

Thankfully, Henny seemed to like Savta. She'd spoken more that Shabbos than she had for the past two days. Though Tehilla wasn't thrilled that she couldn't chat privately with her grandmother when Henny was around, she was relieved that Henny seemed a bit more relaxed. Except when she was near Tehilla.

"Tehilla, you must take Henny to that nature preserve near the shul," Savta said. "I'm sure there's nothing like it in Brooklyn."

"Sure," Tehilla said quickly. She sneaked a peek at Henny. Henny remained impassive.

"I'm going to take a nap," Savta said, rising. "Your mother's cholent always makes me sleepy."

Mrs. Markson looked up from her book and laughed. "Anyone's cholent would make you sleepy."

"True," Savta agreed. "Good Shabbos, ladies."

Tehilla watched her grandmother make her way out of the living room. Her mother was engrossed in a book, while she and Henny were perched at opposite ends of the room, as far away from each other as they could be.

Tehilla sighed. Maybe she'd get to discuss this situation with Henny later, with Savta. Her grandmother's advice was usually right on target.

"Girls, why don't you go to the assisted living facility today?" Mrs. Markson suggested.

"Well, I already told my friends that I'm not coming because Savta's here," Tehilla replied.

"You have plenty of time to go before Savta wakes up," Mrs. Markson said. "Come, I'll walk with you to the Kappels'. I could use some fresh air."

Tehilla glanced sharply at her mother. Was she offering to walk with them to help diffuse the tension between Henny and Tehilla? Henny remained sitting on the couch. "You'll enjoy going to the assisted living facility, Henny," Mrs. Markson coaxed.

"Um, I'm not really in the mood," Henny said listlessly.

"You don't have to be in the mood for a mitzvah," Mrs. Markson said with a smile. "Trust me, you'll enjoy it. The ladies will be thrilled to meet you. It's such a *chessed*."

Henny looked unconvinced, but she stood up.

"Bundle up, girls," Mrs. Markson said as she buttoned her coat. "It's getting nippy outside."

Tehilla sighed as she pulled on her Shabbos coat. She wouldn't have minded if Henny had stayed behind.

"New Rosedale is certainly different from Brooklyn, isn't it," Mrs. Markson commented as they stepped outside. Henny nodded politely. "It took me a while to get used to life here when we first came." Mrs. Markson chuckled at the memory. "We only came here because my husband was learning in the *kollel*. But now...now I wouldn't move anywhere else — well, except for Eretz Yisrael, of course."

"My grandparents live in Eretz Yisrael, but I've never been there," Henny said.

Tehilla eyed her compassionately. It seemed like her closest family members were so far away. Poor girl.

"The girls usually meet at the Kappels' and walk together to the assisted living facility," Mrs. Markson explained as they headed up the walk leading to Shevy and Adina's house.

She knocked on the door. It was pulled open by a little girl.

"Good Shabbos, Mali," Mrs. Markson said. "Is your mother still up? I'll come in for a minute if she is."

Shevy came to the door. "Oh!" she said, looking surprised. "I thought you weren't coming."

"My grandmother took a nap," Tehilla said with a shrug. "So I figured I'd come along."

"You can thank me," Mrs. Markson laughed as she took a seat on the couch beside Mrs. Kappel. "There wasn't much else for these two girls to do, so I kind of pushed them out the door."

Adina came into the living room, followed by a familiar blond girl.

"Kaila!" Tehilla exclaimed. "What are you doing here? Shevy didn't say anything about you coming for Shabbos."

"I'm staying by my sister," Kaila explained.

"Oh, I forgot that your sister moved to New Rosedale," Tehilla said. She'd met Kaila's sister Aliza when Kaila had stayed at the Kappels' house a few months earlier.

"She lives near her in-laws," Kaila said.

"Kaila's sister married Mr. Stepanov's son," Adina told Henny.

"Oh, really?" Henny said politely.

Tehilla watched a giggling Shevy show Kaila a picture of the three Kappel boys with pillowcases tied around their heads.

"Thank goodness they're out of the house this afternoon," Shevy said dramatically, causing Kaila to smile.

Trust Shevy to become good friends with a girl who'd stayed at her house for only a short time. Would the same ever happen with her and Henny?

She doubted it — especially after yesterday's fiasco.

A knock sounded at the door, and Mali ran to answer it.

"Good Shabbos!" they could hear Sara Leah and Penina say.

"Now that everyone's here, let's get going," Shevy said, heading to the coat closet.

"See you later, girls," Mrs. Markson told Tehilla and Henny. "Enjoy yourselves."

Henny didn't look too happy, Tehilla noted.

The walk to the assisted living facility was pleasant, if not a bit cool.

"Mrs. Kanter said she'd be waiting in the lobby for us," Shevy told the girls.

Sure enough, an elderly woman beamed at them from a beige couch in the corner.

"Good Shabbos, girls," Mrs. Kanter said eagerly. "I've been waiting for you since...oh, since last week's visit." The girls giggled as they sat down on a few couches and armchairs arranged in a rectangle.

"Good Shabbos, Aunt Golda," Kaila said demurely.

"Oh, my Kaila!" Mrs. Kanter's eyes lit up. "I'm so happy you came."

"Mrs. Kanter is Kaila's great-aunt," Tehilla told Henny.

Henny looked at her in surprise. Tehilla wasn't sure if that was because of what she'd just said, or because those were the first words the two had exchanged since the previous day.

"I see we have a new visitor today," Mrs. Kanter said, her eyes falling on Henny.

It never failed to amaze Tehilla how although weak in body, Mrs. Kanter's mind was still sharp.

"This is Henny Hart," Tehilla introduced her guest. "She's staying at my house."

"Oh, how nice," Mrs. Kanter said, her eyes creasing behind thick glasses. "How long will you be staying there?"

Henny's eyes darted around, looking trapped. "Um...I'm not sure."

Mrs. Kanter smiled. "Well, however long you stay, I hope you enjoy it. Your friends here are lovely girls."

Tehilla wasn't sure if Henny agreed, but she nodded politely anyway.

"Where are you from?" Mrs. Kanter asked Henny.

"Brooklyn," she responded.

"How lovely," Mrs. Kanter said. "I had a good friend who lived in Boro Park. I used to visit her from time to time on Shabbos. It's nice there, isn't it?"

"Very nice," Henny agreed demurely.

Tehilla noticed that Shevy and Penina were staring at Henny — and they didn't look too happy. Suddenly, she realized what was upsetting them. Most probably Henny had regaled the sixth graders with lots of far-fetched stories about her life in Flatbush — and, like Tehilla, they had a hard time believing them. Tehilla tapped her foot nervously on the carpeted floor. Maybe Savta could give her some ideas how to handle this.

The rest of the visit passed in a blur for Tehilla. She was too preoccupied to focus on the conversation — and too aware of Henny sitting only a few feet away from her. She glanced at her watch surreptitiously, willing the minutes to march on until she could go home and speak to her grandmother.

"Good Shabbos, girls," Mrs. Kanter said when the girls stood up to leave. Then she added, like she did every week, "Come next week, all right?"

"Of course," Shevy answered for all of them.

The girls left the assisted living facility, talking leisurely.

"It's getting chilly, isn't it?" Sara Leah remarked.

"Yeah," Adina replied, sticking her hands in her pocket.

"It was smart of you to wear a warmer coat," Sara Leah said to Tehilla.

Tehilla didn't answer.

"Uh...Tehilla?" she tried again.

"Huh?" Tehilla said, looking around quickly. Had someone just called her name?

"Are you okay?" Sara Leah asked, looking concerned.

"Er...yeah... I mean, why not?" Tehilla flushed. It wasn't like her to be so spaced out.

She fell silent again, trying to pay better attention to the conversation but not quite succeeding. She parted from the other girls in front of the Kappel house and hurried home alongside Henny. Their Shabbos shoes clacked loudly against the pavement, accentuating the lack of conversation between the two girls.

"Um…" Tehilla broke the silence, fumbling for something to say. "How do you like my grandmother?" She blushed, realizing how foolish she sounded.

"Oh, she's so nice," Henny enthused, sounding grateful that Tehilla had broken the ice. "She's so different from my own grandmother, but then again, I hardly see my grandmother."

Tehilla felt relieved as they approached her house.

"Good Shabbos," she called as she stepped into the house. She and Henny hung up their coats in the closet, and then they headed to the kitchen to help Mrs. Markson prepare *shalosh seudos*.

"Good Shabbos," Mrs. Markson greeted the girls. She was busy preparing a salad at the counter.

"Yum," Tehilla said as she watched her mother mix together the ingredients. "That's my favorite salad."

"Savta's too," her mother said. She turned to Henny. "*Shalosh seudos* here is usually a ladies' only affair," she said. "My husband eats *shalosh seudos* in shul."

"My father used to do that, too," Henny said. Tehilla turned around just in time to catch a nostalgic expression flit across Henny's face.

"Good Shabbos," said Savta, appearing in the doorway to the kitchen. "I slept much longer than I'd planned to — and I'm still tired."

Tehilla perked up when she saw her but realized that any private conversations would have to take place later.

"Must be the weather," Mrs. Markson said. "I always feel droopy this time of year, when the weather shifts between cold and warm, and seems to never quite make up its mind."

Savta helped herself to a cup of tea and carried the glass to the dining room. Tehilla and Henny set the table.

"We're all set," Mrs. Markson said, carrying in several platters and a plate of gefilte fish.

Tehilla relaxed slightly when they were all seated around the table. Somehow, with her mother and Savta right there, she felt like everything was going to be okay. At times she felt like a little kid again, believing that the adults in her life had the ability to make things just right. How badly she wished that were true.

"I've waited months to hear you sing '*Mizmor L'Dovid*' again," Savta said, turning to Tehilla with a smile.

Tehilla smiled back. She enjoyed singing just as much as her grandmother enjoyed listening to it, and *shalosh seudos* usually turned into an impromptu concert, starring Tehilla.

Tehilla took a *bentcher* and began to sing. She listened to the sound of her clear voice as it filled the regal dining room, rising and falling gracefully. To her surprise, she heard another voice join in, harmonizing gently with hers. Tehilla faltered a bit as she stared at Henny, who was singing along with her eyes closed. Tehilla glanced at Savta, who was clearly enjoying herself, and her voice gained momentum again. Henny was *good*, she had to admit. She had a beautiful voice, and her harmonies complemented the tune perfectly.

"That was gorgeous," Savta exclaimed when the song wound down to a close.

"Stunning," Mrs. Markson commented.

Tehilla glanced at Henny, who looked suddenly bashful.

"Where did you learn how to sing so well?" Savta asked Henny.

"Well, my father was...is...a *chazzan*." Henny fumbled over her words, and flushed. Tehilla wondered why she'd referred to her father in the past tense. "Singing runs in my family, I guess."

"Just beautiful," Savta said almost to herself, shaking her head slightly. "Girls, how about '*Yedid Nefesh*'?"

"My family used to sing a special tune that my great-grandfather composed years ago," Henny said, somewhat hesitantly. "Do you want to hear it?"

"Please," Savta said eagerly.

Henny closed her eyes again, and Tehilla could see her as she must have looked at home, in her parents' house. Then she began to sing, and Tehilla stared at her in awe.

The song was haunting and majestic, and Henny's voice soared and dipped accordingly. Tehilla remembered how Henny had boasted of all the solos she'd received in school. It was probably true that she'd been assigned solos in abundance. With a voice like that, the choir heads were sure to have taken advantage. Tehilla's heart sank as she realized something. If that story was true, then...maybe some of her other stories were also true? But if that were so, then how was she to know which ones to believe?

Chapter 12

The end of Shabbos was probably the least favorite part of Tehilla's week. It was hard to make that transition from calm peacefulness to hectic, busy days. This week, though, the conclusion of Shabbos meant more than that to Tehilla. It meant her grandmother was going back home. They hadn't had much time during Shabbos to talk, like they usually did. Henny's presence meant that any private time was pushed to the background, in favor of catering to the new girl in the Markson house. Tehilla couldn't help feeling resentful. That was why, when her grandmother smiled at her across the table after Havdalah, Tehilla felt her spirits lift. Maybe she'd help Savta pack her things, and they could have their long-awaited discussion after all.

"*Gut voch*," Rabbi Markson said pleasantly. "A good week, a happy, peaceful week, to all." He looked meaningfully at Tehilla, and she flinched. Was it so obvious to everyone that she and Henny weren't really getting along?

"Tehilla," Savta said, "do you mind...mind..."

Tehilla looked at Savta strangely. Her mouth looked slightly twisted, and her words were slurring together.

"Savta, are you okay?" she asked.

Rabbi Markson looked at his mother in alarm. "Ima, talk to me," he said urgently. Savta simply looked at him, her eyes frightened, for several long moments. Finally, she exhaled, and her face seemed to straighten out.

"I... I... Oh, now I can talk," Savta said, sighing in relief. "That was so strange. But I'm feeling better now, *baruch Hashem*."

The Marksons watched Savta worriedly.

"I need to get in touch with the couple who's driving me home," Savta continued, sounding like her usual efficient self. "They said they'd be leaving about an hour after Shabbos. Tehilla, can you pass me the phone?"

Tehilla held out the phone to her grandmother.

Savta struggled to reach out her arm. "I... I can't..." she mumbled, her mouth drooping and her words barely audible.

Rabbi Markson rushed to her side. "Ima, can you lift up your right arm?"

Savta complied.

"Now try lifting your left arm again."

Savta tried, and couldn't.

"Ima, talk to me."

The left side of Savta's mouth was slack, and she couldn't get any words out.

"I'm taking you to the emergency room," Rabbi Markson said abruptly.

Tehilla gasped. Henny, standing in a corner of the kitchen, looked scared.

"I'm sure it's nothing," Savta protested, when she was able to speak again. "I'll go home, get back to routine, and I'll feel fine."

Rabbi Markson shook his head grimly. "We've got to get you to the hospital," he said. "Just in case."

Savta's shoulders drooped slightly, as if submitting to her son. Tehilla clenched her hands into tight fists. What, exactly, were her parents worried about?

Mrs. Markson ran out of the kitchen and returned a moment later. "Let me help you with your coat, Ima," she said, helping her mother-in-law into her trim peacoat. Savta moved slowly, and Tehilla wondered how her grandmother had suddenly turned into an old woman.

"I'm going to get the car from the driveway," Rabbi Markson told his wife. "Meet me outside — it's quicker that way. The sooner we get there, the better."

Mrs. Markson nodded and led Savta out of the kitchen.

"I'll call you from my cell phone, okay?" She turned around and looked at Tehilla, her eyes compassionate. "It'll be okay. Just *daven*." With that, she disappeared, leaving the house suddenly feeling very empty and quiet.

Tehilla stood in the corner of the kitchen, quivering with fear. Had Savta just been sitting at the kitchen table only minutes before? Had Shabbos really just ended only a quarter of an hour ago? She felt like she'd suddenly been catapulted to a different world, and she had no idea how to regain her footing in it.

"Let's say some *Tehillim*," Henny said, her voice shaking.

Tehilla stared at her, wondering through the fog that had enveloped her brain why Henny seemed so affected. It wasn't like Savta and Henny were particularly close. They'd conversed pleasantly over Shabbos, it was true, but they'd only met two days before.

Whereas Savta was part of Tehilla's earliest memories. Tears filled Tehilla's eyes as she accepted the *Tehillim* Henny offered her. She remembered how Savta would tell her how she said *Mizmor L'sodah* when she was born. "How perfectly your name suits you," Savta would always say. "Our personal *tehillah* to Hashem."

"Please," Tehilla whispered, the words coming out in a gush, "let Savta be okay."

The girls sat side by side at the kitchen table, whispering words of *Tehillim*. Suddenly, Henny looked up.

"What's your grandmother's name?" she asked.

"Huh?" Tehilla stared at her, confused.

"Her *Tehillim* name," Henny explained.

"Oh. Um...it's Dina bas Chava." It felt so wrong to be confining Savta — her capable, spirited grandmother — to a name synonymous with sickness. Savta hardly ever got sick, and she was as self-sufficient as they came. Tears trickled down Tehilla's cheeks. Oh, what was going to be?

The hands on the prominent round kitchen clock noisily made their rounds as the girls continued to *daven*. Tehilla had just closed her *Tehillim* and was staring mindlessly at the wall when Henny spoke up.

"Why didn't your parents call Hatzolah?" Henny asked, her voice subdued. "Do you even have Hatzolah here?"

"What?" Tehilla shook her head, trying to clear it. "Yeah, we do. But, um...the hospital is really close...seven minutes away by car. Anyway, my grandmother seemed fine. I guess my parents weren't in such a big rush." She sounded defensive, almost as if she were trying to convince herself that it were true.

Henny fell silent, looking unconvinced. "Should...should we clean up from Shabbos?" she asked, eyeing the dishes stacked in the sink and the remnants of *shalosh seudos* visible in the dining room.

"Yeah, I guess so," Tehilla said, rousing herself. At least it would give them something to *do*. She stood up, toying with the idea of calling her mother's cell phone. She wanted to speak to her, desperately, but she was scared of what she might hear. What if something was really wrong with Savta, *chas v'shalom?* What then? She squeezed her eyes shut.

"Are you okay?" Henny asked.

No, I'm not, she wanted to say. *My grandmother's in the hospital, and I have no idea what's wrong with her, and why are you asking me this?* Instead, she nodded. "I'm fine," she said tersely.

The room was enveloped in a brooding silence as the girls put away the Shabbos paraphernalia and washed dishes. Tehilla was drying the cutlery when the phone rang. She lunged for it.

"Hello?" she said quickly, her heart beating faster than it ever had.

"Tehilla," came her mother's voice. She sounded so far away.

"What happened?" Tehilla practically shouted. "Where's Savta?"

"Savta seems fine." Tehilla nearly sagged against the wall in relief. "The doctors are running tests on her now. They think she had a ministroke, but they don't know for sure yet."

"A...stroke?" Tehilla gasped.

"It'll be okay, Tehilla. We came to the hospital just in time, *baruch Hashem*...early intervention is very important for stroke victims. The doctors were happy we came in right away."

Stroke victims. Could they really be talking about her beloved *savta* in such cold, clinical terms?

"I'll call you soon, okay?" Mrs. Markson said.

Tehilla felt like throwing up. She groped her way to the kitchen table. She needed to sit down, to feel the solid presence of a chair anchoring her to her spot. Nothing, it seemed, would ever be solid about her life again. Tehilla buried her face in her hands, swaying back and forth. *Savta,* she keened wordlessly. *Savta...*

That's when she heard it. A low, moaning noise emanated from Henny, who'd been standing silently near the kitchen table during Tehilla's telephone exchange. Tehilla turned around to find the younger girl looking pale and drawn, her stricken eyes standing out against the pallor of her face. She was trembling all over.

"Are you okay, Henny?" Tehilla asked nervously.

Henny swallowed hard, trying to calm down.

Tehilla stood up and took a step in her direction. "What's going on?" she asked worriedly. "Are you sick?"

Henny shook her head, still looking scared and wan. "It's just..." Her eyes drooped, then looked straight at Tehilla. "It's just...a stroke..." She swallowed hard. "That's what happened to my father."

Chapter 13

our father?" Tehilla repeated dumbly. Through her stupor she realized that she was awfully close to uncovering Henny's secret, but she was too upset about Savta to even care.

"It was...horrible." Henny covered her face with her hands, as if she could blot out the memories. "I woke up that morning to my mother shouting into the phone that something was wrong...that Hatzolah had better come quickly..."

Her breaths sounded loud and ragged in the quiet kitchen.

"They came...three men running into the house... My

sisters were crying, and I ran into their bedroom and closed the door until the men left...with my father..." Tears stood out in Henny's eyes, and Tehilla felt her own eyes well up. "My mother called to me that she was going to the hospital...she'd ask a neighbor to come over and we should get ready for school..."

"You went to school after all that?" Tehilla asked, amazed.

Henny nodded. "I didn't know what else to do. But it was...the longest day in my life...the worst day ever. I only found out when I came home that my father...he'd had a...a stroke." A few tears spilled onto her cheek, and Henny wiped them away defiantly. She swallowed hard.

"The whole thing was so weird," Henny said, almost to herself. "No one could believe it. My father was way too young to have a stroke."

"That's awful," Tehilla said in a whisper. "I'm so sorry." She hoped that Henny could understand what she really wanted to say: *I'm sorry for the way I've been treating you. I'm sorry I was so quick to judge you...* Guilt and shame flooded her, and she looked down, not wanting to catch Henny's eye.

An awkward silence settled over the two girls, broken only by the shrill ringing of the phone a few moments later.

"Hello?" Tehilla said, grateful to whoever was calling for getting her out of an uncomfortable situation.

"Hi, Tehilla!" came a familiar deep voice.

"Baruch!" Tehilla said. It was her oldest brother.

"You sound strange, Tehilla. Are you feeling okay?"

Tehilla sniffled, and a tear trickled down her cheek. She breathed deeply, trying to gain control over herself, but then... "No," she practically wailed. She knew she sounded like a baby but felt helpless to stop. "I'm not!"

"What happened?" Baruch asked, alarmed.

"It's Savta..."

"What's wrong?" he asked quickly. "Didn't Savta come for Shabbos?"

"She did! But..."

"Tehilla, what's going on? Tell me what happened!"

"I..." Tehilla closed her eyes, allowing the tears to seep out. "She had a...a ministroke...the doctors think... She's going for tests now..."

"A stroke! Are you serious? When?"

Tehilla simply shook her head, then realized her brother couldn't see her. "I can't..."

"You know what? I'll call Mommy myself, okay? Speak to you later, Tehilla."

He hung up, and Tehilla gulped loudly. She peeked at Henny, embarrassed to be blubbering like a baby.

"It'll be okay, Tehilla," Henny said in a subdued voice.

"How do you know?" Tehilla asked, snatching on to her words like a lifeline. Henny was experienced with this kind of thing, it seemed. But, the thought occurred to her, if Henny was staying at their house for so long, then where were her parents?

"What happened to your father in the end?" Tehilla blurted out without thinking. Henny recoiled, and Tehilla felt her heart sink. She had *not* meant to say that aloud.

"He's...away now," Henny said hesitantly.

It's okay, Tehilla wanted to tell her. *You don't have to tell me what happened. Really.*

"His left side was paralyzed," Henny continued quietly. "He needs rehab...for a really long time. His doctors sent him to this place in Texas. There are closer places, but they said this one's the best, so...they went. He's getting better, my mother says. But...it's so far away," Henny finished, her voice sounding muffled. She turned and ran out of the kitchen.

Tehilla stared after her, her stomach knotting. *Great job,* she told herself. *For the second time in two days you make your boarder flee the kitchen.*

The phone rang again, and Tehilla picked it up listlessly.

"Hi, Tehilla," her mother said loudly. "How's it going there?"

Tehilla didn't reply, and her mother didn't wait for her to speak.

"Savta is still undergoing tests... So far so good, *baruch Hashem*. The doctors haven't found any damage. She'll need to stay overnight for now, and we'll see tomorrow what the story is. Hopefully, she'll be discharged after twenty-four hours."

"Are you coming home?" Tehilla wanted to know.

"Not yet," her mother answered. "We're going to stay with Savta as long as we can. I'll call you with an update in about an hour, okay?"

Tehilla sighed. "Okay," she mumbled.

She hung up the phone and looked around the kitchen. It was clean, and traces of Shabbos were pretty much gone. Now what? Was she supposed to go upstairs and comfort Henny, who was most likely crying her heart out? Or was she supposed to wait for Henny to come back downstairs to speak to her? She shook her head. This was too confusing.

"Was that your mother?" said a shy voice.

Tehilla looked up to find Henny standing in the doorway.

"Yes!" she said, relieved that Henny had made the decision for her. "She said that my grandmother seems fine but has to stay overnight at the hospital."

"I'm glad," Henny said, a smile lighting up her pale face.

Tehilla looked thankfully at her. Even though Henny's story didn't have a happy ending — yet — it was nice that she could rejoice with the Marksons.

"Me too," she said, feeling better than she'd felt in a long time — or at least since Henny had first stepped through the Marksons' front door.

Just a few more hours and the nightmare would be behind them. Savta would be released from the hospital later that evening, healthy and whole, and they could pretend the events from last night had never happened.

Tehilla was just about to ask her mother about preparing a welcome home supper for Savta, when the phone rang.

"Hello?" Tehilla said eagerly. She'd been expecting Meira to call.

"Can I speak with Abraham Markson, please?" came a deep, official-sounding voice.

Tehilla was momentarily flustered. "Um...he's not home. Can I take a message?"

"Is there a cell phone number where I can reach him? I'm calling from Stone Hospital."

Tehilla's eyes widened. Savta was staying at Stone Hospital! What was going on? "Ma," she whispered urgently to her mother, who was washing dishes, "it's the hospital."

Mrs. Markson swiped her hands on a dishtowel and grabbed the phone, her hands still damp. "Yes?" she said quickly. A crease appeared between her eyebrows, and her mouth was set in a pinched line. "I'm Abraham Markson's wife... I see... I'm going to get in touch with my husband and we'll be right over..." She hung up the phone and started punching in the numbers.

"Ma!" Tehilla practically cried. "What's going on?"

Mrs. Markson held her finger to her lips while she waited for her husband to pick up.

"Avraham," she said, "the hospital just called... There's something wrong with your mother's blood work... Okay,

I'll be waiting outside."

She hung up and turned to face Tehilla. "I have to run to the hospital," she said quickly, moving toward the coat closet. "It looks like Savta has some sort of infection, and we need to speak to the doctors."

Tehilla gasped. "What..."

"It's okay, Tehilla," her mother said soothingly. "It might be nothing."

"But then why'd they call you?" Tehilla cried worriedly. "They wouldn't have called you to come down for nothing."

"We asked the hospital to let us know right away if anything is wrong," Mrs. Markson explained. "Abba is Savta's only child...she has no one else to take care of her."

"I want to come, too," Tehilla said, grabbing her coat.

"I don't think that's a good idea," her mother replied as she grabbed her black pocketbook and slung it over her shoulder. "Besides, who will stay with Henny?"

Tehilla pressed her lips together. It was always about Henny, wasn't it? Couldn't she have a moment away from the girl? The telephone rang just then, and Mrs. Markson hurried to answer it.

"Hello?" she said breathlessly into the phone. "Right now? Hmm... Hold on a minute and I'll ask them, all right?" She reappeared in the hallway a moment later. "Tehilla, Mr. Berg just called. He needs a babysitter for about two hours while he takes the new baby to the doctor. Can you do it?"

"Right now?" Tehilla folded her arms. How in the world

was she supposed to babysit while her grandmother was lying in some stiff hospital bed?

"He sounds desperate... The baby sounds like he has a cold, which can be dangerous for a newborn."

"Let me find out if Henny is interested," Tehilla suddenly said. She darted up the stairs before her mother could protest.

"Henny," she called as she knocked on the door to their boarder's room.

Henny pulled it open, her eyes questioning.

"Can you babysit at the Bergs'?" Tehilla asked quickly. "You know...that's the family we went to last week."

"When?" Henny wanted to know.

"Right now. They've got to take their new baby to the doctor."

Henny nodded, and Tehilla flew down the stairs.

"Henny can do it, Ma," she called. "She's coming downstairs now. I'll go with you to the hospital, okay? Please?"

Mrs. Markson pursed her lips, thinking for a moment. "Henny, do you mind going to the Bergs' alone?" she asked when Henny came down the stairs at a more sedate pace.

Henny grinned. "Those kids are so cute... Of course I don't mind. I used to babysit all the time."

"*Tizki l'mitzvos*, Henny," Mrs. Markson said warmly. "Here, I'm going to write down my cell phone number for you in case you run into any problems. And take a spare key with you, in case you come home before us, all right?"

Henny nodded and accepted the key and paper that Mrs. Markson had scribbled her number on. "*Refuah sheleimah* to your grandmother," she said to Tehilla.

Tehilla flushed, feeling like she was abandoning Henny. "Thanks," she mumbled.

A honk sounded outside.

"That must be Abba," Mrs. Markson said. She hurried out of the house with Tehilla right behind her.

Tehilla slid into the car, noting right away the tension that filled the car. Her fingers trembled slightly as she thought of Savta. She remembered how her teacher last year had asked their class to take on an extra *zechus* so her father might merit a *refuah sheleimah*. The girls had *davened* for him each morning and had undertaken numerous *kabbalos* in his merit. A *tefillah* for Savta was never far from Tehilla's lips, that was for sure. She'd *davened* with extra *kavanah* that morning and had murmured numerous *perakim* of *Tehillim* throughout the day. Now, she just needed something to do in her grandmother's *zechus*, something that would help her get better. But what?

The car rounded the corner and drove past the Kappel house. Tehilla caught sight of Shevy playing catch on the front lawn with her brothers. A moment later the Kappels were out of sight...but Tehilla sat up straight, her eyes gleaming. Her grandmother needed a *zechus* badly. And she had just the idea of what exactly she could do to help bring one about.

Chapter 14

ow's your grandmother feeling?" Sara Leah asked kindly.

Tehilla sighed. "She's still in the hospital," she said, practically exhaling the words. Tears stung her eyes, and she blinked fiercely. Mr. Stepanov's minivan was not exactly an ideal place to cry. She turned her gaze to the window, unwilling to continue the discussion. Images of Savta, looking tired and pale, lying against the white hospital sheets, filled her mind. Her usual *sheitel* was replaced by a faded snood; her tasteful clothing was gone — in its stead a drab hospital gown. When had her independent, personable grandmother become a wan old lady?

The realization that the grandmother she had always admired was aging hurt. And the knowledge that she might be very sick was agonizing. While Tehilla didn't understand all the medical jargon her parents had tossed about with the doctor, she understood enough to realize that her grandmother's blood tests had revealed an infection — and that the doctors needed to make sure it hadn't entered her bloodstream.

"It may be a false positive," one doctor had explained to Tehilla's parents. "But we can't know that right now. We'll be running another test soon to find out conclusively. Meanwhile, we'll need to keep your mother here for at least another night."

Tehilla felt scared when she saw the apprehension on her parents' faces.

"Tehilla, come here," Savta had called from her bed, her voice an echo of its usual strong tones.

"You look so tired, Savta," Tehilla said, then mentally kicked herself. What a silly thing to say to someone in the hospital.

But Savta had merely chuckled. "Hospitals are not a place to rest, that's for sure. I must have had every test in the book — MRI, echocardiogram, CAT scan, and lots of other things that I can't even name. Not to mention being woken up what seemed like every few minutes to have my temperature and blood pressure taken. I'm beginning to feel like my arm will explode from that machine!"

Tehilla peered at her. There was no indication that her grandmother realized something was wrong. Or maybe she was just a good actress? "Come home soon, Savta," Tehilla said, her voice cracking. Savta had merely squeezed her hand.

"...choir coming along?" Shevy was saying.

Tehilla shook her head, trying to come back to the here and now. She was on her way to school, and Shevy Kappel wanted to know about choir practice. She frowned. Choir practice seemed like it belonged to another world, a world where Savta was well, a world where everything in her life was safe and predictable. Not like the world she lived in today.

"The *melaveh malkah* is really soon, isn't it?" Adina said. "My mother just got an invitation in the mail."

Despite herself, Tehilla felt a jolt of anticipation, followed by a lurch of guilt. Maybe it was wrong for her to feel excited when something was wrong with Savta?

"It's in two weeks, I think," Tehilla said slowly. Actually, she knew that for a fact. At their last practice, Miss Brickstein had stressed that time was running out, and they'd better know the songs perfectly — along with the choreography. They still had to learn the motions for a few songs.

"What about that song you're singing solo, Tehilla?" Penina asked.

"What about it?" Tehilla asked.

"You know it already, and everything?"

Tehilla felt the familiar glimmer of excitement. Of course she knew that song, forward and backward and even in her sleep. Simply put, she couldn't wait for her moment in the spotlight.

"The girls in my class who are in choir are so excited," Shevy remarked. "Lucky them!"

"Oh!" Tehilla said aloud. Her friends all turned to look at her, and she flushed. Shevy's words had made her remember the idea she'd had the day before. Her grandmother was always stressing the importance of *shalom* — between family members, between friends, between all Jews. Something was obviously not going well with Henny and the rest of the sixth grade. Henny was unusually quiet in the car on the way to and from school, and no one from her class ever called to speak to her. Tehilla was determined to make peace between Henny and the sixth grade — and thereby accrue *zechusim* for her grandmother's speedy recovery.

Project Peace. Tehilla smiled proudly to herself. She liked the ring of it. Starting today, she'd invest whatever efforts she could into helping Henny acclimate into her new class. She'd make sure that Project Peace was a success. "Shevy," she said casually, "tell Henny about that brunch your class worked on earlier in the year and how you came up with the craziest theme."

"Oh, that," Shevy said offhandedly. She looped a glittery rubber band around her fingers and then added another one. "It was so long ago. I hardly remember it."

Tehilla shot her a strange look. Shevy usually enjoyed regaling others with one of her many feats. Why, when it came to Henny, did Shevy suddenly clam up?

"Penina, why don't you tell her?" Tehilla urged.

Penina simply shrugged.

A tense silence hung in the air. Tehilla tapped her foot impatiently, wondering how she could help Henny if her classmates were so clearly not interested in having anything to do with her. There must be something else she could do.

"Tova Goldblatt in my class said that her sister is helping Miss Brickstein make up the motions for choir," Sara Leah said, breaking the silence.

Choir. Choir. Choir.

Tehilla pounced on Sara Leah's words, turning them over and over in her brain. Something told her that herein lay the solution to Project Peace...but what, exactly, was it? Finally, as the minivan pulled up in front of Machon Malka Mirtza, Tehilla had her answer. She sailed out of the car, a smug smile playing on her lips.

"Now, all girls standing on the gray tile take a step to your left," Miss Brickstein instructed.

The girls obeyed. Devoiry, trying to follow instructions, toppled right onto the floor. "I had no clue that being in choir meant I had to be a dancer, too," she grumbled good-naturedly. The other girls giggled.

The choreography sure was complicated, Tehilla had to admit. She had no idea how they were going to have all the motions down pat in time for the *melaveh malkah*. But from the way Miss Brickstein was drilling them, it was clear that the teacher had no such compunctions.

"Now, put your right hand forward, like this" — Miss Brickstein pretended to hit an imaginary wall in front of her — "and then follow with your left hand. Bring your hands together, fingers out..."

Tehilla tuned her out. She'd spent the entire choir practice planning in her head what she'd say to Miss Brickstein. Practice was over in only five minutes, and she still wasn't sure how to approach the teacher.

"Now, left together, right together..." Miss Brickstein swayed from side to side, sounding — and looking — like an aerobics teacher rather than the head of a choir. A few girls tittered. "Girls, c'mon!" Miss Brickstein chided, moving faster. "We're going to wow everyone at this *melaveh malkah!*"

The girls began to move a little faster. "And now... Tehilla, are you with us?"

Tehilla blushed. Miss Brickstein was looking straight at her, along with most of the other girls in the room. She nodded her head. "Great...especially since you're standing in the front!"

Tehilla nodded again. She knew that she'd been placed in the front row because of her voice, and she didn't want to risk being relegated to a different position where no one could see her. She pushed all thoughts of the impending conversation out of her mind and tried to focus on the complicated choreography.

"Good job, ladies!" Miss Brickstein crowed. She pushed her hair out of her face and prepared to leave the room. "Keep practicing — at home, in front of a mirror, in front of your families... Let's get this perfect, okay?" She threw her briefcase over her shoulder.

Tehilla approached her quickly before she lost her chance. "Um...could I speak to you for a minute?" Tehilla asked, swallowing nervously. So much hinged on this plan.

"Sure," Miss Brickstein said, giving her a dazzling smile. "I definitely have a minute to spare for my star soloist." She led Tehilla out of the room and to a private corner in the hallway.

"Well...um..." All of the words she'd mentally rehearsed flew out of Tehilla's head, and she was left stammering unintelligibly. Miss Brickstein looked at her encouragingly, and Tehilla managed to find her tongue again. "It's like this," she finally said. "There's this girl boarding at my house...she's in the sixth grade. She has a really beautiful voice... I heard her sing myself. I know it's a little late and everything, but she's having a hard time settling in, and I thought that...well, I thought that maybe joining the choir would help her become a part of things."

Tehilla stumbled over the words, annoyed with herself that she found them so hard to say. She knew that letting Henny's spectacular voice into the choir would likely detract from her own moment in the spotlight. But it would also earn Henny the respect of her classmates — something she needed so badly.

"That's such a lovely idea," Miss Brickstein said. Tehilla smiled hopefully. "But I can't do that right now," the teacher continued. "It's too late to let a new girl into the choir. We've already learned all the songs and harmonies, not to mention most of the choreography."

Tehilla felt deflated. "But..."

"I will definitely keep her in mind for the next choir we put together," Miss Brickstein said briskly. She flashed another smile at Tehilla and strode down the hall. Tehilla stared after her, wondering why everything with her plan was going so wrong.

Chapter 15

our seconds, three seconds, two seconds... Tehilla stared at her watch, waiting for the second hand to strike the tiny black line. *Rrrriiiing!* It was all Tehilla could do to stay in her seat while Mrs. Leibowitz finished assigning that night's math homework. Finally, the teacher dismissed the class and she bolted out the door.

"Where are you rushing to?" Meira asked, looking up from her knapsack.

"I need to catch someone," Tehilla threw over her shoulder. "I'll call you later."

Tehilla rushed to the sixth-grade classroom, hoping the

principal was nowhere in sight. Running was a no-no in the corridors of Machon Malka Mirtza. If only the sixth grade hadn't been dismissed yet. She had no doubts that Shevy Kappel would be one of the first girls out of the classroom, and if the sixth graders had left all would be lost. To her relief, the classroom door was firmly closed and she could see Mrs. Barnet standing in front of the room, speaking as if the day were nowhere near coming to an end.

Tehilla pressed herself against the side of the door, where the teacher couldn't see her. From that angle she had a good view of the classroom. Penina seemed to be listening to the teacher; she was taking notes and nodding her head every so often. Henny, sitting in the back of the classroom, looked bored. She was tapping her feet and sighing every so often. Shevy, sitting in the middle of the room, looked like she was about to leap out of her seat at any moment. Her eyes were darting all around the room, giving the impression of a trapped toad waiting to jump to freedom.

Finally, Mrs. Barnet seemed to have wound down the lesson because the sixth-grade classroom came to life in a rush of chairs scraping back, knapsacks being stuffed with books, and girls making a beeline for the door.

Tehilla was not surprised to see Shevy leaving the room first.

"Shevy!" she called to her.

Shevy looked surprised to find her there. "Hi," she said.

"Shevy, I need to speak to you for a minute." Tehilla steered Shevy down the hall.

"Where are you taking me?" Shevy protested. "We're going the wrong way. Our chauffeur will be here any minute." She grinned, knowing that Tehilla liked to refer to their driver as a chauffeur. Tehilla didn't smile back, though.

"This will be quick," Tehilla said firmly. She looked the younger girl squarely in the eye. "Shevy, I want to know what's going on with Henny. She seems so...unhappy. I know I asked you this once before, and then I told you to forget about it, but I think things are just getting worse."

Shevy looked stonily at Tehilla.

"Really," Tehilla said, "can't anyone have a little pity on her?"

Shevy suddenly came to life. "Pity," she spluttered. "Maybe *she* should have pity on *us* and stop telling us a bunch of lies about how wealthy her parents are or how big her house is!"

Girls were casting them funny glances, and Tehilla led Shevy into an empty classroom.

"You know Yocheved from my class?" Shevy continued, her eyes blazing. "She was telling her cousin that there's a new girl in her class named Henny Hart, from Flatbush. And you know what her cousin said?" She didn't wait for Tehilla to answer. "That Henny lives on her block in a small two-family house, and as far as she knows Henny's parents are not in Europe — and probably have never been there either. So after we found that out, can you blame us for not wanting anything to do with her?"

Tehilla's stomach twisted queerly. No, she couldn't blame them. She'd felt the same way, after realizing that Henny's stories couldn't be true. And yet... "Shevy," she blurted desperately, "what if I told you that Henny's father is sick, and that he's away with her mother for rehab?"

Shevy recoiled, and Tehilla suddenly realized that she'd had no right to share Henny's secret. "Shevy," she said quickly, "please, please...don't tell anyone about this! I don't think Henny wants everyone to know. I think that's why she makes up stories...and also because it makes her forget, for a little, about what's really going on in her life. Or at least to pretend that it's not happening."

It wasn't until she said those words that she'd realized they were true. Henny's stories served as a form of escape for her. It was wrong to fabricate untruths, of course, but what right did they have to judge Henny?

"Shevy," Tehilla tried again, "I really didn't mean to share Henny's personal life with you. I just wanted you to try...to try to accept her, to include her. Things are hard enough for her without being the misfit of the sixth grade."

Shevy was quiet, and Tehilla took that as a good sign.

"She's suffering, Shevy," Tehilla said, sighing. "I'm going to do my part to help her...and I really hope you can do yours."

Shevy didn't say anything more, and the two girls headed quietly outside.

Adina waved to them through the open door of the minivan. "Where were you two?" she asked. "Shevy, you're always the first one outside."

"I got...delayed," she mumbled. "Sorry."

"Me too," Tehilla said as she climbed inside.

She hoped her words had had some influence on Shevy. She noticed that for once, Shevy didn't touch the bags of rubber bands in her knapsack, and she was unusually quiet during the trip home. Was that a good sign or a bad one? She sighed. There was no way to know.

"Hi, Ma," Tehilla called as she stepped through the front door.

"Hi, girls," Mrs. Markson said as she came into the hallway.

"What's new with Savta?" Tehilla asked nervously. She hung up her coat, her fingers trembling slightly.

"*Baruch Hashem*, the doctors said everything looks okay," Mrs. Markson said, sounding pleased. "They're hoping to release her tomorrow morning."

Tehilla sagged against the wall in relief. "*Baruch Hashem*," she whispered. "But Ma," she suddenly realized, "does that mean they don't know what happened to Savta on Motza'ei Shabbos? What if it happens again?"

Mrs. Markson pursed her lips. "Well, she's going to take an aspirin every day from now on — that's supposed to help ward off strokes. But really, Tehilla, the only thing we can do is *daven*."

And gather as many zechusim *for her as we can*, Tehilla added silently. She sighed. If only her beloved grandmother would stay healthy! Tehilla sighed again as she eyed Henny, who was already climbing up the stairs with her knapsack. Helping her acclimate to life in Machon Malka Mirtza was becoming quite a formidable task. Tehilla decided to follow her mother to the kitchen before heading upstairs to start her homework.

"I just spoke to Ari," Mrs. Markson said. "He and Baruch have an off Shabbos this week." Tehilla clapped her hands together excitedly. She didn't see her brothers too often, and she missed them. "It works out perfectly," Mrs. Markson said, "because Henny's aunt called to invite her for Shabbos this week."

Tehilla smiled in relief, then flushed guiltily. She would be as nice to Henny as possible, she really would. But did that mean it was wrong to rejoice over some private family time?

"Is Savta going to stay at our house when she gets out of the hospital?" Tehilla asked, changing the subject.

Mrs. Markson chuckled ruefully. "You know Savta. She wants to be in her own house, in her own four walls. She says she's perfectly fine and will manage on her own."

Tehilla grinned. That sounded more like her grandmother. She tried to superimpose a typical image of Savta

— well dressed and poised — over the weak woman in the hospital bed. Luckily, it wasn't too hard. Hopefully, the events of the past few days would soon be behind them, and they could move on to bigger and better things. Like the choir.

"Ma, did you get the *melaveh malkah* invitation?" Tehilla asked eagerly.

"I did," Mrs. Markson replied. "It's been so busy here, I forgot to mention it. It looks beautiful, Tehilla... I can't wait to attend."

"Can we invite Savta to come also?"

"Of course. She wouldn't miss it for the world. She loved every minute of last year's choir."

Tehilla smiled to herself, relishing her secret. She still hadn't told her mother about the song she'd be singing solo. She wanted it to be a surprise.

"Can I help with something?" a soft voice said.

Tehilla and her mother turned around to find Henny standing in the doorway.

"Sure," Mrs. Markson said. "Do you want to set the table?"

"Okay," Henny agreed, heading to the cutlery drawer.

"By the way, Henny," Mrs. Markson said, "your aunt called before. She wants to invite you for Shabbos."

"For Shabbos?" Henny's eyes clouded over.

"Do you want to go?" Mrs. Markson asked gently.

"Um...yeah. It's just..." Henny sighed. "She probably wants to make a *shalosh seudos* for my bas mitzvah. All the girls in our family have one...all the aunts and girl cousins come, and it's really fun. My mother was thinking of coming for Shabbos, but tickets were too expensive."

She looked so forlorn that all Tehilla could do was gape at her. How horrible! To celebrate such a milestone on her own while her parents were so far away... Mrs. Markson seemed equally perturbed, though she did a good job of masking her emotions.

"Which day is your birthday, Henny?" she asked.

"On Wednesday," Henny replied glumly.

Tehilla and her mother exchanged a quick glance. Mrs. Markson gave a slight nod, and Tehilla realized that her mother was thinking the same thing that she was. They had only two days to put together some type of party for Henny. It was a tall order, and Tehilla couldn't help but wonder if they could really pull it off.

Chapter 16

"What should we do for her?"

Tehilla and her mother were holding a hushed impromptu meeting at the kitchen table. The rest of the house was silent; Henny was probably fast asleep already.

"We can have a nice supper with just the four of us," Mrs. Markson said. "Abba, me, Henny, and you."

Tehilla cocked her head. "I don't know... We're not her family, after all. Maybe she'll think it's weird. Or maybe it'll make her miss her parents even more."

"There's no way I can make a party for her class in such a

short time," Mrs. Markson said. "We can push it off another week, maybe. It doesn't *have* to be on her birthday."

"I doubt they would even come," Tehilla said darkly.

Mrs. Markson looked taken aback. "Why do you say that?"

"They...they don't really like her so much," Tehilla admitted.

Mrs. Markson narrowed her eyes thoughtfully but didn't say anything.

"Why don't we make something here, with just the girls in our carpool?" Tehilla finally said. "They all live close by, so transportation isn't a problem, and Henny knows them already."

Mrs. Markson nodded slowly. "It's not too many girls, so cooking for them won't be hard," she said. "But it's enough girls to make the gathering feel more festive. Fantastic idea, Tehilla!" Tehilla looked pleased. "I'll go shopping tomorrow, after Savta gets out of the hospital, and cook on Wednesday morning," Mrs. Markson said. "We'll serve a refreshing fruit cup for an entrée, some salads, the sweet-and-sour meatballs that Henny likes together with rice, and I'll make some type of mousse for dessert. If I have extra time I'll make small knishes as another side dish." Mrs. Markson scribbled on her notepad, clearly in her element.

"We should probably get pretty paper goods," Tehilla said. "Something that will look fancy, and that's different from the dishes we usually use. Oh, and a present!"

"I'll take care of that," Mrs. Markson said, making some more notations.

"Great," Tehilla said, satisfied.

"You'll tell the girls in your carpool, right? Maybe we should surprise Henny...tell them not to talk about it in front of her."

Tehilla's stomach lurched. She would tell the other girls, of course, but something told her that Penina and Shevy wouldn't come so willingly — if at all. Shevy was still acting distant toward Henny, even after Tehilla had spoken to her. She'd have to find a way to get them to her house, without revealing the real reason why she was inviting them. She sighed. This was all so complicated.

"Good night, Tehilla," her mother said, standing up. "It's late, and we've got lots to do over the next few days." Tehilla stood up and stretched. She walked together with her mother toward the staircase. "I'm proud of you, Tehilla," her mother said, turning suddenly to look at her. "I know it isn't easy for you to have Henny stay here. You're doing a terrific job."

"Thanks," Tehilla said, squirming uncomfortably. She hadn't been doing such a good job so far, but she was determined to make up for it.

"Hi, Adina," Tehilla said as she sauntered down the school halls the next day. "Can I speak to you for a minute?"

"Sure," Adina said. She followed Tehilla to a quiet corner to escape the recess din.

Tehilla opened her mouth to speak, then quickly closed it again. She'd been about to invite Adina to Henny's bas mitzvah supper, but wouldn't Adina tell Shevy? And if she asked Adina to keep the invitation under wraps, wouldn't that sound odd? Adina was looking at Tehilla strangely. Tehilla flushed, suddenly not sure what to say. "Um...actually, I wanted to ask you something."

"Yes?" Adina said politely.

"Well, I need help with something at my house tomorrow night, and I was wondering if you could come over about half an hour after school..." She trailed off, realizing how strange that sounded.

Adina looked surprised. "I don't see why not. I guess I could ask my mother."

"Great!" Tehilla enthused. Her mind raced quickly. Should she ask Adina to relay the message to Shevy? They were sisters, so chances were they'd be arriving at her house together. She decided to risk it.

"Maybe Shevy can also come?" she ventured. "Um... I'm going to need *lots* of help."

"What's the problem?" Adina asked.

"Well..." Tehilla thought quickly. "It's hard to explain. You'll see when you come over, okay?"

"I guess so," she said. "Do you need both me and Shevy? My mother usually needs our help around then."

"Yes!" Tehilla said loudly, then flushed. "I mean, yes... I need both of you." What would she do if Mrs. Kappel vetoed that, she wondered desperately. She'd have to ask her mother to call and explain the situation. Who ever knew it could be so hard to plan a simple supper? She almost laughed at the irony of the situation: The supper was supposed to be a surprise for Henny, but here she was driving herself crazy trying to keep it a surprise from her guests, too! Adina was still peering at her.

"I'll tell you all about it tomorrow after school," Tehilla finished brightly. She waved and then dashed down the hall, leaving a confused Adina staring after her.

"Oh, hi, Penina!" Tehilla said as she almost crashed into the younger girl.

Penina pushed her blond hair out of her eyes and smiled at Tehilla. "Actually, it's a good thing I bumped into you," Tehilla said. "I wanted to talk to you." She took Penina by the elbow and steered her to an empty classroom. "I need your help with something tomorrow night, at my house," she said.

"Tomorrow night?" Penina repeated. "My mother doesn't really let us go out at night. She likes when we do our homework and get to bed on time."

"Oh, it won't take long," Tehilla said, pasting a wide smile on her face. "And I really, really need your help — and Sara Leah's, too."

"Sara Leah?" Penina frowned slightly. "Why do you need both of us? I don't think my mother —"

"I'll take care of your mother, okay?" Tehilla said,

mustering all her self-control to appear cheerful and calm. She made a mental note to ask her mother to call Mrs. Kappel and Mrs. Steinberg. She doubted anyone would understand why this surprise dinner had to be kept a surprise from the guests, too, but it was too complicated to explain. The whole thing was starting to give her a bad headache.

Penina shrugged. "What do you need help with anyway?"

"It's hard to explain," Tehilla said, parroting the line she'd used with Adina. "Anyway, recess is almost over. See you later!" She gritted her teeth as she made her way back down the hallway to her classroom. She passed Adina on the way, who was still looking at her strangely. Tehilla merely smiled thinly and held her head high. No one said this was going to be easy. But why did it have to be so hard?

"Hi!" Tehilla chirped brightly as she hopped into the minivan at the end of the day. Her stomach clenched. What if Adina or Penina mentioned how Tehilla had invited them over the next day? Then all would be lost. She couldn't let that happen. She had to keep talking to make sure no one let anything slip.

"How was your test?" she asked Sara Leah.

Sara Leah looked blankly at her. "What test?"

Tehilla bit her lip. "Didn't you have a test today?"

Sara Leah shook her head. "Nope, but I've got one tomorrow."

"Well, then, *I* had a test today," Tehilla prattled. "Well, it wasn't really a test. It was more like a quiz. But I studied for it like a test because it was sooo hard. You better watch out, Shevy and Penina, for next year. You're not going to know what hit you."

"Hmmm," Shevy murmured absently. She was busy making yet another rubber-band keychain.

Tehilla took a sip from her water bottle, and Adina took the opportunity to speak up. "I heard the choir sounds stunning," she commented.

The choir. That was a safe topic to talk about.

"It does," Tehilla agreed. "It's absolutely amazing how Miss Brickstein pulled it all together. Each song is so gorgeous, and the harmonies are out of this world. And the chore-ography...you'd think we were all professional dancers or something."

She paused for air, and Penina spoke up. "What did you — "

Tehilla's eyes widened in alarm. Penina couldn't be asking about tomorrow night, could she?

"I mean," Tehilla said quickly, interrupting Penina mid-sentence, "last year's choir was also unbelievable. Remember it from last year's assembly?" She didn't wait for her friends' nods. "But I think this year's choir is going to be even better. I really, really can't wait for it."

Somewhere during her monologue Tehilla realized that her friends were looking at her strangely. She shrugged slightly, as if to tell herself that it was okay. She was doing this for Henny's sake. It would be unbelievably awkward if Shevy and Penina found out about tomorrow night's supper and refused to come. Henny would realize right away what was going on. There was no way she could let that happen. When she'd exhausted the topic Tehilla switched to a new one — the recent clothing sale held in the Kuntlers' basement.

"And all the clothing was straight from the stores in Brooklyn, only much, much cheaper," she gushed. "They had this stunning two-piece outfit, but it was already sold out in my size. Mrs. Kuntler offered to ask her cousin — she's the one who owns the store in Brooklyn — to get it in for me, but then I... Oh!" Tehilla stopped mid-sentence and clapped her hand over her mouth.

"What's wrong?" Adina asked.

Tehilla didn't answer. She'd just remembered that her friends needed to show up at her house attired appropriately. It wouldn't do for them to come to a bas mitzvah celebration in their uniforms. And what about the guest of honor herself? How could she persuade Henny to get dressed accordingly if the party was a surprise? How was she going to figure this one out?

"So what happened?" Shevy asked, looking up from her rubber bands.

"Huh?" Tehilla stared blankly at her.

"Did they ever get in that outfit for you?" Shevy asked curiously.

"What outfit?" Tehilla had no recollection of what she'd been talking about.

"Are you okay, Tehilla?" Sara Leah asked anxiously.

"Yeah, I'm fine, just fine," Tehilla mumbled.

She hugged herself nervously as her thoughts tumbled all over each other. This party was presenting more and more obstacles each minute. And she had to figure out what to do about it — fast.

Chapter 17

The first thing Tehilla noticed when she stepped through the front door was that the house was quiet. Too quiet.

"Ma?" she called tentatively.

There was no answer. She turned around to face Henny. "Did my mother say she's going somewhere?" she asked.

Henny shook her head. "Not that I know of."

"Girls?" Mrs. Markson called. She pushed open the front door, her keys jangling in her hand, and smiled wearily. "You beat me home."

"Where were you?" Tehilla asked, taking some grocery bags out of her mother's hand.

"I had to drive Savta home, and then I had to do some shopping."

"How's Savta feeling?" Tehilla asked, making a mental note to call her grandmother later that evening.

"She's fine," her mother said. "A bit tired, but happy to be home."

Tehilla followed her mother to the kitchen, while Henny headed upstairs.

"Did you go shopping for the party?" she asked, riffling through the grocery bags.

Mrs. Markson shook her head and turned to look at Tehilla. "Actually, Tehilla, we can't make the party after all."

"Why not?" Tehilla said quickly.

"I was speaking to your principal today, and I mentioned that we're making a supper for Henny. She told me that it's against school policy to invite only some girls in the class to a bas mitzvah party."

"But Henny's not really part of the school," Tehilla protested. "And her bas mitzvah is so soon and we didn't even know about it! Besides, it's not a party — it's a supper."

"I know," Mrs. Markson agreed. "Mrs. Levitan understands that, but she wants us to follow the school's rule anyway. She also thought it would be better if we made Henny a class party. She says it'll help Henny integrate into her class — and I think she's right. We can make a party for Henny's class next Sunday. It'll be easier for the girls to get here on Sunday than during the week."

Tehilla shook her head miserably. "They won't come, Ma."

"I don't know about that," Mrs. Markson said thoughtfully. "I'll speak to their teacher and Mrs. Levitan... I hope we can work something out. I think it's important to do this for Henny, so she shouldn't feel so different from everyone else."

Tehilla realized belatedly that her mother must have been speaking to the principal about Henny in the first place. "Won't Henny feel bad if she knows you've been speaking to everyone about her?"

"She'll never find out," Mrs. Markson said. "If their teacher decides she needs to speak to the class I'm sure she'll send Henny out of the room on some pretext or another."

Tehilla merely shrugged. That was probably true, but still...

"We can invite Henny's aunt, and her sisters," Mrs. Markson continued. "And it would be so nice if all of the girls in your carpool can come too."

Don't count on it, Tehilla thought darkly. The chances of Shevy and Penina attending were next to nothing. And the chances that their classmates would travel to New Rosedale for a party in honor of Henny Hart were even slimmer.

"Maybe we should keep the party a surprise," Tehilla said. "I mean, just in case no one comes she won't be disappointed."

"They'll come, Tehilla," her mother said patiently. "Don't worry so much. But a surprise might be a good idea.

Actually, since there really isn't enough time to make invitations and mail them out, we should call the girls ourselves — and that way Henny won't find out that we're making it in the first place." She flicked open her notepad, looking businesslike. "We can serve some salads and desserts, just like we did at your bas mitzvah," she said, scribbling quickly. "And of course, we'll need to plan some type of project." She looked thoughtful as she considered the possibilities.

Tehilla exhaled, feeling the tension of the past few days catch up to her. All her subterfuge had been for nothing. There would be no nice, small bas mitzvah supper. Instead there would be a big party, which no one would show up to. This was one huge disaster in the making.

To tell or not to tell? Tehilla's head ached from considering the question. All the girls in the sixth grade were bound to find out sooner or later about the bas mitzvah. Tehilla guessed that after Mrs. Markson spoke to their teacher, she would lecture the girls about the importance of attending — and would tell them to keep it a surprise. Still, maybe it would be better if she informed Shevy and Penina beforehand?

"Tehilla Markson! Are you with us?"

Miss Brickstein was looking at her accusingly. Tehilla blushed and nodded. "Let's go then!" Miss Brickstein instructed.

"We've got to get the motions for *Sim Shalom* down pat. The *melaveh malkah* is only days away!" Tehilla snapped to attention. "Smile, girls!" the teacher commanded. "Remember, we want the audience to think you're enjoying yourselves!" She laughed. "Because you are!"

"Really now?" a voice muttered dryly behind Tehilla.

Tehilla smiled to herself. Choir rehearsals were beginning to resemble an aerobics workout, and though its members were gifted with sweet voices, many of them had two left hands and feet.

"Pick your hands up to the sky, as if you can touch it!" Miss Brickstein commanded, marching in place. A few girls groaned.

"I can't move my feet and my hands at the same time — not to mention sing!" Yael Katz protested, sounding flustered.

"Practice makes perfect!" Miss Brickstein said, flashing an encouraging smile. "Forget about singing for now. Just move those hands and feet."

"I thought we were a *choir*," Shira Levy grumbled.

"Okay, girls," Miss Brickstein said, dropping her hands to her side. "That was wonderful. Tonight, I want you to practice, practice, practice all those motions we learned today. I want you to know them in your sleep!"

"I won't even remember them in five minutes," Yael said mournfully.

Miss Brickstein didn't seem to hear. She waved to the girls and rushed out the door.

"I don't remember last year's choir being like this," Tehilla said thoughtfully.

"Me neither," Devoiry agreed. She sighed. "I wonder if we'll really have this all down pat by the *melaveh malkah*."

"I hope so," Tehilla murmured as she sidled out the door. The halls were quiet; classes were in full swing. She was almost by her classroom door when she saw a familiar figure heading her way. "Shevy! What are you doing here?"

Shevy grinned. "I needed a short break."

"Recess was only half an hour ago," Tehilla said, looking pointedly at her watch.

Shevy shrugged. "Half an hour is a long time."

"Actually, Shevy, if you're not in a rush..." Tehilla thought quickly. She may as well confide in Shevy before she found out the news a different way.

"My mother wants to make Henny a bas mitzvah party on Sunday," she whispered. "It's a surprise, so please don't say anything." She expected Shevy to storm away, or flatly say that she wasn't going to come. Instead, to her shock, Shevy's eyes gleamed.

"Great!" she enthused.

"Great?" Tehilla echoed questioningly.

"I love parties!" Shevy gushed. "They're so much fun!"

Tehilla didn't know how to react. It would have been nice if Shevy was thrilled for Henny's sake, but she couldn't ask for more right now. Maybe with time everything would change.

"What are you doing at the party?" Shevy asked eagerly.

"I'm not sure," Tehilla admitted. "My mother thinks we should make some type of project."

"Adina made something gorgeous at a bas mitzvah once," Shevy said. "She still has it hanging in our room. Maybe you can —"

"Girls!" came a stern, familiar voice.

"Uh-oh," Shevy muttered, not daring to turn around.

Tehilla turned pale as she looked up at the principal's dark eyes.

"Girls, please get back into class," Mrs. Levitan said. "Choir practice is over."

Later, Shevy mouthed to Tehilla as she headed back to her classroom. Tehilla nodded slightly as she walked down the hall. She tried to stifle the smile that threatened to take over her face. Never had she dreamed that Shevy would come on board so willingly. And knowing Shevy, she'd be able to convince her classmates to attend the party as well. Maybe, just maybe, it wouldn't be such a flop after all.

Chapter 18

*J*t's going to be just perfect," Tehilla said happily.

"I'm glad it's all working out," came Meira's voice over the phone.

"Me too. Henny's already left to her aunt for Shabbos, and she won't be back until Sunday morning — just in time for the party." Tehilla giggled. "Her aunt said not to worry...she'd make sure that Henny came dressed up, without telling her the real reason why. And Henny's other aunt is bringing her sisters, so she'll be *really* surprised!"

"Wow, that's really kind of you, Tehilla," Meira said.

Tehilla brushed off the compliment. "The Steinbergs and

Kappels are coming over on Motza'ei Shabbos to help set things up, and Sunday morning we'll take care of the finishing touches. I can't wait to see Henny's face!"

"I wish I could see it, too," Meira said. "But my mother won't let me miss the next gown fitting — and it's called for the same time as the party."

"I'll take lots of pictures," Tehilla assured her. "I want to make a scrapbook for Henny after the party, or maybe some type of poster with photos, so she can show it to her parents."

"She'll be thrilled," Meira said.

"I hope so," Tehilla said. She was about to say something else when the doorbell chimed.

"Gotta go!" she said quickly. "Have a good Shabbos!"

She slammed down the phone and raced down the stairs. She hadn't seen her brothers in what felt like *forever*. She threw the front door open eagerly.

"Tilla!" Baruch exclaimed, falling back on Tehilla's nickname. "How are you?" He put his duffel bag down on the floor.

Ari followed his brother into the house, his suit bag draped over his arm. "Hi, Tehilla!"

Tehilla beamed. "Hi!"

Mrs. Markson appeared in the hallway, smiling from ear to ear. "Oh, you two keep getting taller!" she cried.

"I don't think I've grown in three years," Baruch said with a grin. "But the same can't be said of you," he added, turning to Tehilla. Tehilla smiled.

"Come, boys," Mrs. Markson urged her sons. "You probably want to eat something."

"You bet we do," Ari said, following his mother to the kitchen. "Isn't that why we came home?" He grinned. "Just kidding."

Mrs. Markson cut up hot potato kugel and placed it on the kitchen table. She busied herself with cutting up a marble cake and pulling a bag of chocolate chip cookies from the freezer.

"I forgot to defrost these before," she told Baruch. "I know they're your favorite."

"Thanks, Ma," Baruch said appreciatively. "There's nothing like your food."

"So," Ari said, looking up from his second piece of kugel, "what's it like to have a new sister, Tehilla?"

Tehilla bristled. "I do not... I mean, Henny is very nice and everything but she's *not* my sister!"

"It must be strange to have another girl living here," Baruch said contemplatively. He put a piece of cake on his plate. "I mean, strange for you, Tehilla. I can't imagine having to share my parents with another kid when I was only in seventh grade!"

Tehilla looked gratefully at her brother. Somehow, Baruch always managed to understand her.

"Yeah, it's weird," she admitted. "We're actually making a bas mitzvah party for Henny this Sunday," Mrs. Markson said. "Tehilla's been quite busy all week helping me put it together."

"Nice, Tehilla," Baruch said between bites of cake. "That's a great way to make her feel welcome."

"It's also nice that we won't be around for it," Ari said, helping himself to a third piece of kugel. "Our ride back to yeshivah is leaving on Motza'ei Shabbos."

"Oh, you," Tehilla said chidingly.

"Who's coming to the party?" Baruch asked.

"Most of her class, I think," Tehilla said, looking at her mother. "Right?"

Mrs. Markson nodded. She'd spoken at length with the sixth-grade teacher, and although Tehilla didn't know exactly what she'd said, or what the teacher had told the class, most of the sixth graders had called to confirm they were coming.

"How's Savta feeling?" Baruch asked. "I called her last night, but she wasn't home."

"She seems okay," his mother replied. "She's actually coming for Shabbos next week."

Tehilla's eyes widened. "Really?"

"Isn't next week the long awaited *melaveh malkah*?" Mrs. Markson asked, smiling. "It made sense for her to come for Shabbos, and then she'll come along with us to the *melaveh malkah*."

Tehilla was about to reply when she heard the front door open. A few moments later Rabbi Markson strode into the kitchen.

"*Shalom aleichem*," he said, smiling broadly.

Baruch and Ari rose to greet their father, and Mrs. Markson prepared another plate of food. Tehilla smiled to herself, enjoying the feeling of the whole family together. Somehow, it made her feel so complete. She thought fleetingly of Henny, who was most likely already ensconced in her aunt's house. Her heart constricted in pity. Poor Henny. She would probably give anything to be together with her own family.

"These paper goods are stunning," Sara Leah commented as she opened a package of plates.

"Everything about this party is stunning," Adina laughed. She arranged a stack of napkins on the table and stepped back to admire the effect.

"Your family really knows how to throw a party," Shevy commented, moving energetically around the Marksons' basement.

"My mother took care of the food shopping," Tehilla said. "And we have lots of things — like these fake flowers and fancy bowls — that my mother lends out for *simchos*. So it wasn't like we needed to do too much."

"Still, how did you put manage to put this all together in such a short time?" Adina marveled.

"It really wasn't such a big deal," Tehilla said. "I got the sixth-grade class list from the secretary, and I invited everyone by phone. Shevy gave us the idea for a project, my mother did the shopping and baking..."

"What's everyone going to do at the party, besides for the project?" Shevy asked.

Tehilla was taken aback. "Um... I really don't know. You know, I really didn't think about that. I guess I just figured that by the time everyone shows up and eats something, it'll be late enough. We'll do the project and then it'll be time for everyone to go home."

"You need something else," Shevy said. "What if everyone's done eating really quickly, and the project takes them ten minutes, and then they're all standing around bored?"

Tehilla exhaled sharply. "I didn't think of that," she admitted.

Shevy pursed her lips thoughtfully. "It doesn't matter. There's still a whole night before the party. I'll come up with something to do, don't worry."

Tehilla looked sharply at her. She *was* worried. Who knew what type of far-fetched idea Shevy would hatch up?

"Did you invite Kaila?" Penina asked as she smoothed down a dark pink tablecloth.

"Oh, I totally forgot about her!" Tehilla smacked her palm to her forehead. "Do you think I should invite her? She only met Henny once, and it's not like the two of them hit it off or anything."

"Of course we need to invite her," Shevy said indignantly. "She was part of our carpool, too, even if it was just for a short time. And besides, it would be nice for her to see the girls in my class again."

"The party's tomorrow," Adina pointed out. "How can you invite her so late?"

"I'll call her right now!" Shevy said. "Tehilla, may I use your phone?"

Tehilla pointed to a phone hanging on the basement wall. "Go right ahead."

Shevy punched in some numbers and waited for the phone to ring.

"Hi!" she said cheerily a moment later. "It's me... I mean, it's Shevy Kappel... May I please speak to Kaila?"

She waited a few seconds.

"Hi, Kaila! How are you? Great... I'm actually calling to invite you to a party at Tehilla Markson's house tomorrow... Do you think you can get here for it? Remember Henny, that girl who came with us to visit Mrs. Kanter last week? Yeah, her... Anyway, we're making a surprise bas mitzvah party for her at eleven o'clock... I know you don't really know her, but the girls from my class will be there and I thought you might want to see them... Okay... Fine, bye."

She hung up and faced her friends. "She said maybe. Her parents want to visit her sister tomorrow, so they'll be in the neighborhood anyway."

Tehilla nodded and turned her attention to the long

table set up along the wall. She wanted every detail to be perfect. She cast a critical eye over the stack of plates, adjusting them slightly. Then she straightened a few flowers, removed non-existent specks of dust, and moved over a pile of cups.

Mrs. Markson came down the steps, her shoes clattering loudly.

"The room looks magnificent, girls," she exclaimed.

Tehilla looked around appraisingly. It really did. There were bunches of pink balloons in every corner, pink silk flowers as centerpieces along the table where the sixth graders would eat, and a large white armchair designated for the guest of honor. Penina and Shevy had decorated it with pink streamers.

"I'll put out the food first thing tomorrow," Mrs. Markson said. "But I think we're done for now, girls."

"Except for the game," Shevy put in.

"What game?" Mrs. Markson wanted to know.

"The girls might be bored if there's only a project," Shevy said. "I'm going to make up a really fun game for everyone to play."

Mrs. Markson looked at her. "What kind of game do you have in mind?" she asked warily. Tehilla smirked to herself. So her mother was also concerned about letting Shevy concoct one of her outlandish ideas.

"I'm not sure yet," Shevy admitted. "Maybe Penina and I will work on one together."

"That sounds nice," Mrs. Markson said, not sounding so sure of that. "Just run it by me first when you come over tomorrow, okay?"

Shevy nodded, her eyes already glazing over. Her mind was clearly hard at work, mulling over the possibilities.

"Shevy," Tehilla said in a low voice. She motioned to her friend.

"What?" Shevy asked, her eyes refocusing slightly.

"Can I speak to you for a second?"

Shevy followed Tehilla to the far side of the basement, where they could have some privacy.

"I just wanted to thank you for getting involved in all this," she said simply.

Shevy grinned. "I told you already — I love parties!"

"But still..." Tehilla paused, not sure how to voice her thoughts. "I know that you weren't so happy with Henny..."

Shevy's expression suddenly turned serious. "I kept thinking about what you told me, Tehilla," she said. "About Henny's father being sick...about how we can't judge her. And I feel bad for her, really I do. Plus our teacher gave us a whole speech about being more welcoming and all that."

"In front of Henny?" Tehilla was appalled.

"Nah, she sent her out of the room to deliver something to the office."

"That's good. Anyway, I hope she likes this party."

"Oh, she will," Shevy said, rubbing her hands together. "Especially once she sees the surprise I planned for her."

Tehilla was instantly on the alert. "What surprise?"

Shevy pretended to zip her lips. "You'll find out tomorrow, along with everyone else."

"Please, can't you tell me now?" Tehilla knew she was begging, but didn't care. She had to know what Shevy had up her sleeve.

Shevy merely grinned and shook her head. Then she sauntered off to rejoin the other girls, leaving Tehilla staring dejectedly behind her. She could only hope that Shevy Kappel wouldn't do anything to ruin this party.

Chapter 19

Shevy crept into the Markson house, a large bag swinging from her hand.

"Hi," she whispered loudly. Adina followed behind her, looking bemused.

"Hi," Tehilla greeted her friends. "Did you lose your voice, Shevy?"

"What?" Shevy straightened up, looking confused. "Why would you think that?"

"You're whispering," Tehilla replied. "And you're walking kind of funny, too, like you hurt your back."

"She's just in surprise party mode," Adina said wryly. "You know, sneaking around, talking in a low voice..."

Shevy elbowed her sister in the ribs and headed to the basement stairs. "I'm going to dump this in a corner down there, okay?"

Tehilla nodded and led Adina to the kitchen. Mrs. Markson was hard at work mixing salad dressings. "Good morning," she greeted Adina. "Want to cut some cakes?"

"Sure," Adina said, eyeing the platters spread all over the counter. "Wow, these are really pretty."

"I've collected them over the years," Mrs. Markson remarked as she poured a creamy dressing over a bowl filled with lettuce. "Some were gifts, some came along with *mishloach manos*, others I bought on sale…"

The doorbell rang, and Tehilla went to the door. She pulled it open to reveal Sara Leah and Penina, their cheeks flushed and their blond hair slightly windblown. "Come in," she said. "We're in the kitchen, finishing up with the food."

Sara Leah held up the bag in her hand. "My mother sent over some cookies."

"That's so sweet," Tehilla said. "But you should see the spread downstairs. There's enough food to feed the whole sixth grade for a week!"

"When's everyone coming?" Penina asked.

Tehilla checked her watch. "They should be here in another twenty minutes, and Henny's aunt should be bringing her another twenty minutes after that. I really hope your friends come on time so the surprise isn't ruined."

They walked into the kitchen just in time to see Mrs. Markson pull a large box out of the fridge.

"What's that, Ma?" Tehilla asked curiously.

"You'll see in a minute," her mother said, smiling mysteriously. She opened the box and pulled out an enormous, rectangle-shaped cake. It was covered in white frosting and pink flowers. "*Mazel tov, Henny*" was emblazoned in pink across the cake.

"That's gorgeous!" Adina gasped.

"You made that?" Shevy gaped.

Mrs. Markson nodded. "I took a cake-decorating course years ago. I like to try my hand at these things once in a while."

Tehilla looked proudly at her mother. She was really going all out to make Henny happy. "When did you make it?" she asked. "I didn't see you working on it."

"Last night, after you were fast asleep," Mrs. Markson replied. "I didn't have a chance to get to it beforehand, and I wasn't sure it was really happening until I actually got started on it."

"It's going to look stunning in the middle of the table," Sara Leah remarked. "And the pink icing matches the tablecloths perfectly!"

Mrs. Markson laughed as she picked up the cake and carried it downstairs.

Shevy clapped her hands together excitedly. "This is going to be some party, Tehilla!"

"And the cake is just the icing on top," Adina said with a grin. Her friends cracked up.

"Let's bring these salads and platters downstairs," Tehilla said, peeking at the clock. "The sixth graders should be here soon."

The girls trailed down to the basement. Mrs. Markson was giving the room a final, cursory glance. "We did it, girls," she said, smiling. "It looks great."

"*You* did it, Ma," Tehilla countered. "This wouldn't have happened if not for you."

Mrs. Markson was about to answer when the doorbell sounded upstairs. "I think that's our first guest," she said.

"Can I answer the door?" Shevy asked eagerly.

Mrs. Markson nodded, and Shevy bounded up the stairs.

"We forgot to ask her what type of game she planned," Tehilla suddenly realized.

Mrs. Markson's eyes widened. "You're right," she said. "I'll ask her when she comes back downstairs."

Shevy didn't come down the stairs so quickly. The quiet murmur of a few voices in the front hallway quickly swelled to loud chatter as more and more sixth graders arrived.

Mrs. Markson looked at her watch. "They should start coming downstairs," she said. "Henny should be here pretty soon."

"I'll go get them," Penina offered. A few minutes later a group of giggling girls came down the stairs.

"Hello," Mrs. Markson greeted them, smiling warmly.

"Hi," Tehilla said, feeling slightly awkward. It felt strange to be hosting a party for someone else's class on her own turf.

Shevy came down the stairs, slightly breathless, with Kaila trailing behind her. "I think most of the class is here already," she announced.

"Hi, Kaila," the other girls greeted her.

A smile lit up Kaila's face. She hadn't seen the other sixth graders since her short stint at Machon Malka Mirtza.

"I'm so happy you could make it," Tehilla told her.

"Me too," Kaila said demurely. "It's so good to see everyone again."

The doorbell rang again, and Shevy turned back to the staircase. "Sounds like more girls are here," she said.

"Let me get it," Mrs. Markson said, striding toward the staircase. "It's just about time for Henny to arrive. Why don't you girls quiet down while I go see if it's her?"

Mrs. Markson turned off the basement light on her way up the stairs, and the room was plunged into darkness. The girls immediately quieted down, punctuating the silence with hushed whispers and nervous giggles. Footsteps sounded on the stairs.

"She's coming!" someone whispered loudly.

The girls stood still and waited with bated breath.

"Let me turn on the light for you," they heard Mrs. Markson say. "These steps are a little steep."

The basement was flooded with light. There was a clatter

of footsteps…and then Batya Hoch, followed by Hadassah Schon, appeared in the basement.

"Are we late?" Batya asked, looking around at the faces staring bemusedly at her.

"We thought you were Henny," Yocheved said, tittering.

The girls standing near her started to giggle. Tehilla exchanged a wry smile with Adina. What was with these sixth graders? They were always laughing about something or another.

The doorbell sounded, and once again the basement was thrown into darkness. The girls stood very still, listening to the sound of Mrs. Markson's shoes clacking their way to the front door.

"Oh!" they could hear Mrs. Markson say. "It's so nice to meet you!"

Tehilla strained to catch some more words. Was that Henny at the door? Several moments later the lights were turned on and a woman wearing a dark brown *sheitel* made her way downstairs, followed by three little girls, dressed in matching outfits, who looked like smaller versions of Henny.

"Henny's sisters!" Tehilla said loudly.

The woman, who must have been Henny's aunt, smiled broadly. "That's right. We got a little lost on the way, but we're here just in time."

The three girls huddled around their aunt as if they were an appendage to her. Tehilla's heart went out to them. The sight of so many girls crowded into the basement must have been overwhelming.

The doorbell rang again.

"I'm going to close the light again," Mrs. Markson called down. An instant later the room was dark.

"It's okay," Tehilla could hear Henny's aunt whisper soothingly to her nieces. "Henny will be here soon, and then the lights will go on again."

The room was quiet as Mrs. Markson made her way to the front door.

"Hello," Mrs. Markson said loudly. "We missed you this Shabbos, Henny!"

"She's here," Shevy said in a hushed voice, in case it wasn't obvious.

There was a sharp intake of breath, and the girls stood motionless, waiting. Tehilla clenched her fists together, not sure why she suddenly felt nervous. What if Henny didn't like the party? What if the sixth graders weren't so friendly to her? What if the whole thing flopped and everyone was bored and wanted to go home?

Then she realized something. They'd never had a chance to see which game Shevy had prepared! Tehilla whimpered as she cradled her head in her hands. Who knew what Shevy Kappel had up her sleeve? This whole party was spiraling out of control, and it hadn't even begun.

"What's taking so long?" someone whispered loudly.

They could hear Mrs. Markson talking, and another lady answering her.

"Nechie," Mrs. Markson said, "I'm so glad you brought along your adorable children. Why don't you stay a few minutes and let them play? Henny, can you run down to the basement and bring up a few toys?"

There was silence as the girls waited anxiously for Henny to make her appearance. Tehilla stepped forward, eager to record the moment on her camera. Someone switched the light on, and Henny clambered downstairs.

"SURPRISE!"

Henny jumped back, her hand on her mouth. Her eyes widened as she took in her classmates, and then her aunt surrounded by her sisters.

"I... I..." She moved her mouth, but no words came out.

"Mazel tov, Henny," her aunt said, breaking the silence. She went over to give Henny a hug. Henny just stood there stiffly.

Tehilla watched her nervously. Was she okay?

"I don't believe this," Henny finally murmured. She held out her arms to her sisters, and they tumbled into her embrace. Tehilla blinked quickly and snapped another shot. It made a touching picture.

Mrs. Markson came down the stairs, smiling, followed by Henny's Aunt Nechie, who had three small children in tow.

"Gorgeous party," Aunt Nechie said approvingly, looking around the room. "Henny," she added with a wink, "you never brought up those toys for the kids!"

Henny smiled shyly, and a few sixth graders laughed. "I don't believe this," Henny said again. She blinked a few times and looked around the room in awe.

"Believe it," Mrs. Markson said. She steered Henny to the decorated armchair. "This is your day," she said. "Enjoy it."

Sara Leah turned on some music, and the sixth graders suddenly seemed to come to life.

"Girls, help yourselves to some food," Mrs. Markson instructed. Henny's cousins were already standing near the food, helping themselves to cake and nosh.

"Kids," their mother told them, "just take one piece of cake and come sit down."

Tehilla glanced at Henny, who was still looking around in disbelief.

"When did you do all this?" she asked no one in particular.

"Well," Mrs. Markson said, "Tehilla helped out a lot, and the girls in your carpool came over last night to help set up."

Henny caught Tehilla's eye. "Smile!" Tehilla instructed. Henny flashed a wide smile, which Tehilla duly recorded with her camera.

"Look at this cake," Yocheved announced. "Shevy said Tehilla's mother made it by herself."

Henny stood up and made her way to the food table. She sucked in her breath as she admired the cake. "Is it true?" she asked Mrs. Markson. "You made this yourself?"

Mrs. Markson grinned. "I'll teach you how to do it some-day, if you want."

Tehilla felt a slight pang, but then straightened up. Sharing Henny with her mother didn't mean that she was losing out, she told herself firmly.

Smile at her, she could hear Savta say. *Encourage her... help her...*

She walked over to Henny. "Mazel tov, Henny," she said.

"Thank you," Henny said sincerely. She smiled shyly, and Tehilla understood that she was thanking her for much more than the party.

"You're welcome," she said simply. And she meant it.

Chapter 20

*T*ehilla watched the sixth graders mingle together with satisfaction. Henny looked so happy. Her youngest sister sat on her lap while she chatted with her classmates. She looked more relaxed than Tehilla had ever seen her.

"Maybe we should start the project?" Mrs. Markson murmured in Tehilla's ear.

Tehilla looked at her watch. Enough time had passed since the girls had arrived and eaten. She just hoped the project would take up another large chunk of time so there'd be no need for Shevy's game. She nodded at her mother.

"Okay, girls," Mrs. Markson said, clapping her hands. The sixth graders looked up expectantly. "I think we're about ready to start our project."

Sara Leah and Adina helped roll up the pink plastic tablecloths and put down clear ones in their stead. Tehilla walked around the room, handing each girl an oval mirror. Her mother placed bowls filled with flowers, paints, sequins, and beads on the tables.

Tehilla looked at her mother, who nodded at her. She cleared her throat. "We're going to be decorating mirrors today," Tehilla said. "You can hang these mirrors in your lockers or in your rooms, or wherever you want. You can write your name on them, glue on whatever you'd like... you get the picture."

"Such a cute idea!" Batya Hoch chirped.

"It was actually Shevy Kappel's idea," Tehilla said.

Shevy grinned. Henny looked surprised.

The room lapsed into a pleasant hum of conversation as the girls busied themselves with the project. Mrs. Markson conversed with Henny's aunts. Tehilla sat with Adina and Sara Leah.

"There are extra mirrors," Tehilla told them. "You want to make one?"

"No, thanks," Adina said. "We've been there, done that with these bas mitzvah parties."

"But I think this is the nicest one I've ever been to," Sara Leah chimed in.

"Me too," Adina agreed, looking around the room. Her eyes fell on Henny, who was busy gluing down some flowers. "I mean, I've been to fancier ones, but this one is special, you know what I mean?"

"Yeah," Tehilla said, her throat suddenly feeling thick. "I think I do."

Tehilla watched the girls work on their mirrors. Some of the girls were starting to finish up, she noticed. She glanced at her watch and panicked. They needed to do something else to fill the time. She looked over at Shevy, who was busy telling a story that had the sixth graders doubled over in laughter. She bit her lip nervously. There was no telling what would happen if Shevy introduced her game to the group.

"Can I see your mirror, Henny?" Yocheved called.

Henny flushed and held up her handiwork.

"That's really beautiful," Mrs. Markson remarked, standing up to get a better view. Henny had glued together a few sprigs of flowers, which she had attached to the top of the mirror. She'd written her name in fancy lettering on the bottom, and made a thin border out of sparkly sequins.

"Thank you," she said.

"Speech, speech!" Shevy crowed, cupping her hands around her mouth. "The bas mitzvah girl usually says a *dvar Torah*."

"That's all right, Shevy," Mrs. Markson said smoothly. "This was a surprise, after all, and I don't think Henny is prepared to say one."

"I do want to say something," Henny suddenly said, much to everyone's surprise. She flushed and looked down at the mirror in her hands. "I mean..." She paused and took a deep breath. "I want to say thank you to the Marksons, for letting me stay here. And thank you to Aunt Nechie and to Aunt Chava, for coming to this party and for all that they're doing for my family. And..." No one made a sound. Even Henny's little cousins were quiet. "...thank you to my class-mates, for giving me another chance." The words came out in a soft rush. "I'm going to keep this mirror in my locker so I always remember this party. My teacher last year used to tell us that when we look in the mirror, we should do so proudly. We need to stay true to the type of people we want to be, and remember *who* we want to be. And she always told us that if we made a mistake, we should pick ourselves up and say, 'I'm sorry.'" Henny looked nervously around the room, then back at the mirror in her hands. "And I'm glad I had the chance to do just that." Those last words came out in almost a whisper.

Tehilla looked around the room. The sixth graders looked awestruck. Her mother had tears in her eyes. Henny's aunts were crying softly into pink napkins. Suddenly Tehilla knew just what they should do for the duration of the party.

"*Tov l'hodos la'Hashem*," she started to sing. She motioned to the sixth graders to come join her on the carpeted floor. Sara Leah and Adina came to sit beside her. Tehilla noted with satisfaction that Shevy was sitting beside Henny, her arm around her. Kaila sat on Shevy's other side, looking like she was enjoying herself.

Tehilla sang loudly, her sweet voice leading the *kumzitz*. Henny's voice chimed in with hers, soaring easily over the high notes. The sixth graders looked at Henny in amazement. They continued to sing, Tehilla and Henny's harmonies intertwining and causing Henny's aunts to keep dabbing their eyes.

Song followed song, and Tehilla sang with all her might, realizing that this day would forever change Henny's experience at Machon Malka Mirtza. It would change her, too, she realized, and she was suddenly glad that Henny Hart had entered her life.

"Gorgeous, girls," Mrs. Markson cut in after some time had passed. "I hear some cars honking upstairs. I think some of your parents might be here to pick you up."

"Wait!" Shevy said, jumping up quickly. "We didn't give Henny her surprise." Before Tehilla had time to fret, she was back at Henny's side, holding her voluminous bag. "Here," she said, pulling out a small, gift-wrapped box. "This is our present to you."

Henny accepted it shyly.

"Open it," Batya Hoch commanded.

Henny looked at Shevy, who nodded. Henny tore open the flowered paper and found a small shoe box. She lifted the lid and started to laugh.

"What is it?" Tehilla asked curiously.

"Key chains," Shevy said proudly. "We all made Henny rubber-band key chains."

"That's a lot of key chains," Mrs. Markson observed.

"It's a sixth-grade fad," Tehilla whispered to her.

"Thanks, everyone," Henny said, looking pleased.

"It's also a kind of welcome gift," Shevy said earnestly. She suddenly looked embarrassed. "In case we didn't do it right the first time around."

"Quick, everyone," Tehilla said. "Stand next to Henny. I want to take another picture."

The sixth graders clustered around Henny, grinning broadly. Tehilla quickly snapped another picture. A car honk sounded outside.

"C'mon, girls," Mrs. Markson said. "We don't want to keep your parents waiting."

The girls drifted upstairs, crowding around Henny.

"I didn't know you could sing like that," Yocheved marveled.

"I didn't know you could sing at all," Shira commented. "It's a shame you couldn't be part of choir."

"Yeah," Shevy agreed. "With a voice like that you would've been given a major solo, that's for sure."

With a voice like that...a major solo...

Tehilla flinched, feeling as if she had been physically punched, as an idea occurred to her. Why hadn't she thought of it before? True, she'd asked Miss Brickstein if Henny could join the choir, but this...this was different. And Tehilla wasn't even sure she wanted to think in that direction.

The last of the girls left, leaving behind only the Steinbergs, Kappels, and Henny's aunts with her sisters and cousins. Mrs. Markson closed the front door with a sigh of relief. "Oh!" she said, turning to Henny. "I forgot all about our gift to you. I meant to give it to you at the party, but it slipped my mind."

She headed to the kitchen and came back a minute later holding a slim, gift-wrapped box. Henny opened it to find a pink leather-bound *Tehillim.*

"Oh, it's beautiful," she cried. "Thank you so much! I can't wait to call my mother and tell her all about this party. It was amazing."

"It really was," Adina said, heading down to the basement. "I'm going to start cleaning up down there." Her friends followed behind her.

Tehilla watched as Henny opened up the *Tehillim* and read the inscription that Mrs. Markson had penned inside. Her mother had shown it to her the night before.

We are privileged to have you stay at our house! Wishing that all of your tefillos *should go straight up to* Shamayim *and be answered speedily.*

"Amen," Henny whispered. When she lifted her eyes, they looked slightly damp.

"That *kumzitz* was something else," Aunt Nechie commented, in an attempt to lighten the mood. "It's so special that both Tehilla and Henny can sing — they can harmonize together all the time!"

Mrs. Markson laughed, but Tehilla smiled weakly. Her words only cemented the idea that was fermenting in her brain — an idea that she wasn't even sure she could go through with. She turned to go down to the basement, suddenly feeling as if all the sparkle had drained out of the day.

CARPOOL CLAN

Chapter 21

*H*onk! Honk!

"I'm coming," Tehilla called frantically. "Henny, can you tell Mr. Stepanov that I'll be there in a minute?"

"Yeah!" Henny's reply wafted up the stairs.

Tehilla gritted her teeth in frustration. She just had to brush her hair and make herself look somewhat presentable. She sighed as she ran the brush through her hair with hard, abrupt strokes. She was so *tired*. She must have pressed the snooze button on her alarm clock about six times that morning. And now she was late, late, late

— and she was going to make everyone else late, too.

Tehilla ran out of her room and down the stairs, frowning. Of course she was tired. She hadn't been able to fall asleep until the wee hours of the morning. She was always like that when she had a big decision to make — and this one was as hard as they came.

"Here, Tehilla," her mother said, holding out a brown paper bag. "I packed your lunch and some snack. There's a yogurt for breakfast, too."

"Thanks, Ma," Tehilla said gratefully. She wiggled into her jacket, slung her knapsack over her back and accepted the bag.

"Have a great day," Mrs. Markson said.

"You too," Tehilla replied as she sprinted out the door.

"Sorry," she said as she clambered into the minivan. "I overslept this morning."

"It happens to all of us," Sara Leah replied.

Shevy grinned. "At least I'm not the only one this happens to!"

Tehilla merely sighed as she tried to relax in her seat. "Shevy," she said, remembering something. "My mother found your bag downstairs, when we were putting away the tables after the party. It's still in the basement."

"Oh!" Shevy said. "That was for my game."

"What game?" Henny wanted to know.

"Shevy planned a game for your party, but we never got around to playing it," Tehilla explained. *Thank goodness for that*, she silently added.

"What *was* your game?" Sara Leah asked.

"Nothing too major," Shevy replied. She was busy looping yet more rubber bands around her fingers. "The same game of charades that we played at Penina's bas mitzvah a few months ago. I wanted to come up with something more original but couldn't think of anything."

"Oh, that was a cute one," Penina said, smiling. "We had such a great time."

Tehilla also smiled, shaking her head in wonderment. So she'd made herself frantic for nothing. Still, the *kumzitz* had been the perfect touch to the bas mitzvah. Then she frowned. Except that it had raised a very unsettling thought — and she still wasn't sure what she was going to do about it.

She leaned back in her seat and watched the scenery pass by in a blur. She still had time to think some more.

"Can you believe the *melaveh malkah* is so soon?" Devoiry asked as she walked alongside Tehilla to choir practice. Tehilla shook her head. The thought made her feel excited, but nervous, too.

It was recess, and the halls were crowded with noisy girls. As they passed the sixth-grade classroom, Tehilla felt gratified to see Henny standing outside it, talking to a classmate. The bas mitzvah party had been a good idea.

She knew, though, that Henny still had a ways to go before she truly fit in to her new school. And there was something she could do about it, if only she had the courage…

"…you know what I mean?" Devoiry was saying.

"Huh?" Tehilla had no idea what she was talking about.

"Didn't you hear what I said?" Devoiry was looking at her strangely.

Tehilla blushed. "Um…no, I didn't, sorry."

Devoiry was about to repeat herself when she caught sight of Miss Brickstein waving to them from the doorway of the classroom where choir rehearsals were held.

"Come, girls," Miss Brickstein said in her usual energetic manner. "Everyone else is here already, and we want to get started." Tehilla and Devoiry hurried inside and stood at attention. "Okay, girls!" Miss Brickstein said, clapping her hands. "We're on the last homestretch — just a few more days to go! Today, we're going to start practicing with…" She looked around the room, drawing out the suspense. "…music!" She beamed. "So come, let's head down to the auditorium for a *real* rehearsal."

The girls followed her excitedly through the hallway and down a flight of stairs. Their upcoming performance loomed before them, finally taking shape and form.

Mrs. Katz, the music teacher in the lower grades, was already there with her keyboard. Beside her was another woman they didn't recognize, sitting in front of a set of drums.

"Today," Miss Brickstein said, "we're going to work on singing along with the music — when to begin singing, when to wait for musical interludes...that sort of thing. We're not going to be singing on stage today — just put yourselves in your usual rows, and forget about choreography for now."

"Hurray," Yael muttered. Tehilla, standing beside her, grinned.

"This," Miss Brickstein said, motioning to the music teacher, "as I'm sure you know, is the wonderful Mrs. Katz, long-time music teacher at Machon Malka Mirtza." The girls tittered. Miss Brickstein's effusive introductions were, quite simply, funny. "And this," Miss Brickstein continued, waving her hands to the woman beside the drums, "is one of my very good friends, Mrs. Shonheim." Both women smiled at the girls. "All right, let's go," Miss Brickstein said. "Tehilla, come stand up here. I want to begin with your song."

Your song. Tehilla swallowed hard, suddenly feeling the prick of tears behind her eyelids. She wanted so badly for this song to remain hers alone...but was that the right thing to do?

Miss Brickstein counted to three on her hand, and the music started up, its haunting melody filling the room and seeming to fill Tehilla's whole being. At the signal from her teacher, Tehilla began to sing. She closed her eyes, concentrating on the words, relishing the feeling of being the center of attention.

"Beautiful!" Miss Brickstein said as the song came to a close. "Great job, Tehilla!"

Tehilla gave a small smile as she stepped back. The rehearsal proceeded with song after song, but Tehilla's mind was somewhere else entirely even while her voice sang along.

Finally, they reached their finale song, about a young girl, separated from her mother by war, who describes watching her mother light Shabbos candles. The lilting lyrics described the girl's intense yearning for her mother. Tehilla's eyes flooded with unshed tears when they reached the chorus.

Please keep me by your side,
Just you and I together.
And I'll stay right there with you,
Forever and ever.

Images of Henny kept popping into her mind: Henny sharing how her father was sick, Henny running out of the kitchen, Henny pretending that her parents lived in a mansion... The girl was so unhappy. She missed her parents so much.

Tehilla's thoughts flitted to Savta. Maybe what she was about to do — what she felt she should do — could serve as a *zechus* for her grandmother.

The music picked up in crescendo, and Tehilla sang the chorus along with the rest of the choir. For the first time since yesterday afternoon, she felt some measure of peace.

She'd finally made a decision — and even though it was agonizing, she knew it was the right one.

"Amazing, girls!" Miss Brickstein gushed upon the rehearsal's conclusion. "Tomorrow we'll meet at the same time, but down here in the auditorium. We'll be practicing on stage — with choreography."

"Another exercise session," Yael grumbled.

The girls standing near her giggled, but Tehilla didn't even hear her. She took a few steps toward the teacher, who was already walking away. "Miss Brickstein?" she said hesitantly.

"Yes, Tehilla?"

"I wanted to ask you..." She felt a strange sense of déjà vu as she remembered how she had asked Miss Brickstein to allow Henny to join the choir. She tried to focus on the here and now — convincing the teacher to give Henny something that would mean so much to her.

"Remember I told you about that girl, Henny, who's boarding at my house?" Tehilla tried again. She saw a glimmer of recognition in the teacher's eyes, and she forged on. "Well, I know it's too late for her to join choir, but I was wondering..." She was suddenly gripped by a sense of panic. What was she doing? How could she give away something she'd been dreaming about for so long? Miss Brickstein's dark eyes were upon her, and Tehilla fumbled for what to say next. "I was wondering if I could share my solo with her," she finished in a small, uncertain voice.

Miss Brickstein was quiet, and Tehilla held her breath, not sure what she wanted to hear the teacher say. That of course Henny could sing along with Tehilla? Or that it was too late to even consider such a possibility? What she did, in fact, hear was not at all what she'd expected.

"Wow, Tehilla," Miss Brickstein said, her tone hushed. "I am so impressed with you."

Tehilla looked down at her black patent leather shoes.

"Not everyone would be willing to share her solo to make someone else happy," Miss Brickstein said. "The way you're looking out for this girl and trying to help her is very special."

Tehilla flushed as she met the teacher's gaze.

"I'm willing to try Henny out and hear how she sings," Miss Brickstein said. "She can't, obviously, join the choir so close to the performance, but it might be possible for her to come on stage just for one song, and then go off stage again. I'll think about it."

Tehilla nodded, suddenly happy that she'd worked up the courage to ask Miss Brickstein to give Henny a chance. "I'll let you know my decision tomorrow, okay?" Miss Brickstein said. "And since this goes against my usual policy when it comes to choir, please don't discuss this with anyone." Tehilla nodded again.

"And Tehilla," Miss Brickstein added, her tone suddenly

soft. "I'm guessing that this wasn't an easy thing for you to consider. But I want you to know something."

Tehilla looked at her expectantly.

"If Henny does end up singing with you, you won't be losing your moment in the spotlight," the teacher said. "You'll only be sharing it."

Chapter 22

"How come you didn't say anything, Henny?" Shevy demanded. Before Henny had a chance to answer, she turned to Tehilla, who was sitting beside her. "And what about you? Why'd you keep it a secret?"

Tehilla realized right away what Shevy was talking about. "We just found out about it today ourselves, right, Henny?"

Henny nodded, a smile breaking out on her face. "Remember when Miss Brickstein pulled me out of class yesterday?" she asked Shevy. "She wanted to hear me sing, but she didn't tell me why. Then today she had me and Tehilla sing together, and she told us that we're going to sing Tehilla's song as a duet at the *melaveh malkah*."

Her eyes shone with happiness, and Tehilla smiled to herself.

"I bet someone in our class told Miss Brickstein that you can sing," Shevy said contemplatively.

Tehilla didn't say anything. Let Henny think that someone had mentioned her singing talent by chance. This was one secret she was going to keep to herself.

"Your mother will be so proud when she sees you two singing together," Penina said.

"Actually," Tehilla said slowly, "I never told my mother about the solo. I wanted to surprise her." She turned to Henny. "So don't say anything to her, okay?"

Henny winked conspiratorially. "Okay."

"Miss Brickstein wants me to teach the song to you tonight," Tehilla said. "My mother has to go out for a few hours, so we'll do it then."

The minivan, which had been cruising along, suddenly came to a stop. Shevy peered through the front window and groaned. "Traffic," she stated. "Lots and lots of it."

"There must have been an accident on the highway," Adina muttered.

"I hope everyone's okay," Sara Leah said quietly.

The line of cars stretching in front of them seemed endless.

"I hope this doesn't take much longer," Shevy said,

sounding like her usual self. "We should tell them that we've got two famous singers in the car who shouldn't be kept waiting."

Her friends chuckled.

"Remember when that old station wagon broke down and we were standing on the shoulder of the highway?" Penina asked, giggling. "And Shevy..." She was laughing so hard she couldn't continue.

"That really happened?" Henny asked.

"Sure did," Shevy said, eager to tell the story over in her own inimitable manner. The rest of the trip passed with the girls regaling Henny with stories about their trips to school when Mr. Stepanov's car had been out of service.

Tehilla was still laughing as she stepped out of the car and wished her friends a good night. It only struck her when she was heading up the walk to her house that only a week ago Henny had sat in the car, uncomfortable and quiet. Things had changed so quickly — and she couldn't be more grateful.

"Let's go, girls!" Miss Brickstein instructed. "Take your places, please. We're going to be rehearsing on stage today."

Tehilla headed to her spot on stage in the front row. She watched Mrs. Katz and Mrs. Shonheim, hands perched over their keyboards and drums, and Miss Brickstein, clapping her hands for attention. Henny was standing off to the side of the stage, waiting to come on stage to sing with Tehilla.

Mrs. Katz played a few notes on her keyboard, and the girls fell silent, waiting. Miss Brickstein held up her hand, signaling to them to start singing, and they opened their mouths with gusto.

Miss Brickstein pointed to her lips, reminding the girls to smile during this rehearsal. "Get used to smiling when we practice," she always said. "This way you'll remember to smile for the real thing."

Tehilla stretched her lips into a broad grin, enjoying the sensation of performing on stage. It was the beginning of recess, and from the corner of her eye she could see girls wandering into the auditorium to watch.

The music for the first song wound to a close, and Miss Brickstein looked meaningfully at Tehilla. It was time for her to approach the microphone. Although she'd practiced this song more times than she could count, she felt the familiar nervous twinges. She walked slowly to the front of the stage. She could see Henny make her way onto the stage and stand in front of a second microphone.

The haunting, lilting melody began to fill the room, and Tehilla and Henny started to sing. Tehilla looked at Miss Brickstein, who was clearly enjoying the effects. There was no doubt about it — their two voices were stunning together, sounding even more breathtaking than had Tehilla been singing alone.

Tehilla closed her eyes slightly, allowing her voice to soar and mingle with Henny's. When the last notes of the song had died down, there was a moment of silence in the auditorium. It was broken by the sound of girls clapping and cheering.

"Tehilla! Henny!" came a voice that sounded like it belonged to Shevy Kappel.

Tehilla opened her eyes. There was a large crowd of girls clustered in the room, watching the rehearsal. Henny walked off stage and was immediately surrounded by a crowd of admirers. She accepted compliments with a shy nod of her head, her eyes shining, and Tehilla smiled. No longer would Henny Hart remain a faint shadow on the backdrop of Machon Malka Mirtza. Tehilla's idea had helped her find a niche in her class and in the school.

The music for the next song started up, and Tehilla kept on smiling. As she stood there on stage, preparing to belt out the next song, she realized that Miss Brickstein was right. By giving up her moment in the spotlight, she'd only ended up gaining. And for that, she was truly thankful.

Chapter 23

*T*ehilla's stomach seemed to knot itself tighter and tighter with each passing streetlight.

"Excited, girls?" Mrs. Markson asked from the front seat.

"Yeah," Henny said, just as Tehilla replied, "I'm so nervous!" They both burst into laughter.

"It's really wonderful that Henny was allowed to join the choir on such short notice," Savta remarked. "Although after they heard Henny sing, I'm sure that wasn't a hard decision!"

Tehilla and Henny exchanged a meaningful glance. They'd told Mrs. Markson that Henny wasn't singing for the whole performance. She — and Savta — still weren't aware that Henny was only coming on stage for one song, and that she'd be singing it with Tehilla. Tehilla rubbed her hands together in anticipation.

"I wish my mother could be there," Henny said wistfully.

"I'm going to record the whole thing," Mrs. Markson said. "And we're going to take lots of pictures. Do you have a solo, Henny?"

Henny was taken aback. "Er...no, I don't."

She looked at Tehilla, and the two girls stifled their giggles. Henny didn't have a solo, it was true, but she had something far better.

Mrs. Markson fell silent as she concentrated on the road. It was dark, and Tehilla relaxed slightly as she watched the many lights outside the window winking to her. There was something about the nighttime view, with its sparks of electricity glittering all over, that she found comforting. The car turned off the highway, then turned down the familiar side streets that looked so different at night.

"We're here," Mrs. Markson said finally. She parked the car and they walked toward Machon Malka Mirtza together. Flocks of women, elegantly attired, were heading in their direction.

Tehilla felt a thrill. Soon, these women were going to be watching *her* on stage, listening to her sing and clapping their approval. It was an exciting — and scary — thought.

"Beautiful," Savta murmured as they stepped inside the auditorium. Tehilla looked around, admiring the effect.

Round tables, set up in the center of the room, were draped in silver tablecloths with shiny black cutlery. Large buffet tables, similarly decorated, were strategically placed around the room. A black backdrop had been hung across the stage, and the regular burgundy curtains had been replaced with silver ones.

"Tehilla! Henny!" a familiar voice called.

Tehilla looked up to see Miss Brickstein heading their way. She was wearing a fancy black suit, the highest heels Tehilla had ever seen her in, and her trademark smile.

"Come, girls," she said, motioning them to join her. "We're going to get ready now." She turned to Mrs. Markson and Savta. "I hope you don't mind if I borrow my two star singers," she said.

"Not at all," Mrs. Markson murmured, smiling. "Savta and I are going to sit down at a table near the stage," she told Tehilla. "You can look for us there if you need us."

Tehilla nodded her head as she followed Miss Brickstein to the small backstage room. It was already filled with nervous, chattering girls. They were dressed in black blouses and black skirts, as per Miss Brickstein's instructions. An unfamiliar woman was busy pinning silver sashes around their waists.

"I have two more here, Ima!" Miss Brickstein said, propelling Tehilla and Henny forward.

Tehilla and Henny exchanged a glance and smiled. So the woman was Miss Brickstein's mother. That was so cute! Tehilla watched her curiously. She looked like an older version of her dynamic daughter — shoulder-length *sheitel*, big smile, and a friendly personality.

"Come get your sashes, girls," Mrs. Brickstein said, looking up.

Tehilla stepped forward and watched as Mrs. Brickstein deftly pinned the sparkly sash on her.

"When you have your sashes, come over here," Miss Brickstein called.

The rest of the choir girls were already clustered around her. Tehilla grinned at Devoiry, who had a solo in the first song. "Nervous?" she asked.

"A little," Devoiry admitted. "I mean, all the teachers are here, not to mention about a thousand ladies…"

Tehilla smiled. Devoiry tended to exaggerate.

"Girls," Miss Brickstein said, looking around at the junior-high students, "it's almost time for us to go on stage." She paused, letting the words sink in. The girls swallowed hard, looking serious.

"Mrs. Baum, the head of PTA, is going to speak first and welcome everyone," Miss Brickstein continued. "Then Mrs. Levitan is going to speak, and after that is…our turn!"

Tehilla felt her stomach flutter and suddenly wished she could fast-forward to a few hours later, when this would all be over.

A woman's voice sounded on the microphone, welcoming all the ladies to the *melaveh malkah*.

"Oh, that's Mrs. Baum!" Miss Brickstein said, clapping her hands together eagerly. She suddenly seemed not much older than her students. "Shhh, girls, they can hear us back here. We've got to keep it down."

The girls fell silent, and Mrs. Baum's voice echoed through the room. Tehilla allowed her thoughts to wander. She looked at Henny, who had a serious expression on her face. Henny suddenly sidled over to Tehilla.

"I just realized something," she said in a whisper. "If your mother calls my mother on her cell phone, my mother can listen in to the song."

"That's a great idea," Tehilla said. "Go ask my mother right now."

Henny's eyes darted around. "But... I don't know if Miss Brickstein will let me leave the room." She looked hesitantly at the teacher.

"Do you want me to ask her for you?" Tehilla asked kindly.

Henny nodded, looking relieved. Tehilla walked over to Miss Brickstein and relayed Henny's request. Miss Brickstein looked thoughtful, and then she smiled widely. "I have an even better idea!" she said. "I'll have my mother call on *her* cell phone. This way you won't need to disrupt the speeches." She cocked her head. "In fact, I hear Mrs. Levitan speaking right now." She quickly headed over to her mother and whispered in her ear. Mrs. Brickstein nodded, and her daughter motioned to Henny to join them.

"Henny," Miss Brickstein said, "it's almost our turn on

stage. Call your mother's number now, and my mother will take over, okay?"

"Okay, thank you," Henny said, a smile lighting up her eyes. She punched some numbers into the cell phone and waited for the call to connect.

"Hi, Mommy?" she said after a few seconds. "It's me... I'm at the *melaveh malkah*. How's Abba feeling? ...I'm glad... Mommy, do you want to listen in to the choir? The song I'm singing with Tehilla is the second one..."

She handed over the phone to Mrs. Brickstein a moment later. "Here," she said. "Thank you so much... I really appreciate it."

"My pleasure," Mrs. Brickstein said, smiling warmly.

Tehilla, standing off to the side, was touched.

A few minutes later Mrs. Levitan's speech wound to a close, and they could hear clapping.

"It's our turn," Miss Brickstein whispered loudly. "The curtains are drawn, girls. You have about three minutes to put yourselves in your rows. Make sure you're standing perfectly still, with your hands behind your backs, when the curtains go up — and smile! *Hatzlachah*, girls."

She disappeared, to take up her post at the foot of the stage. Tehilla followed the other girls onto the stage, her heart beating wildly. She turned around to look at Henny, who was waiting in the wings.

"Good luck," Tehilla whispered.

"You too," Henny replied, smiling nervously.

Tehilla slipped into her spot and stood tall, her hands behind her back. Strains of music began to waft through the air, and the curtains were slowly pulled open. The room was dim, and Tehilla blinked from the glare of the spotlight. As she started to sing, her eyes grew accustomed to the brightness, and she could make out a table right in front of the stage, filled with teachers and the principal. At a table to the left, she could see her mother and Savta, beaming proudly. Weeks of rehearsals had culminated in this moment. It was all so surreal.

The first song passed in a blur of practiced motions and upbeat harmonies. Tehilla's heart hammered as the strains of the song died down. She saw Miss Brickstein looking at her, and she walked slowly to the microphone. From the corner of her eye, she could see Henny make her way to the second microphone. Then the music started, sweet notes that tugged at the heartstrings. Tehilla could only make out the women in the front of the room, and their eyes were focused on her and Henny. She could see her mother and Savta, who were watching intently.

She half-closed her eyes, concentrating on the melody, and started to sing. Her voice soared along with Henny's, their harmonies captivating the audience. Suddenly, Tehilla wanted this moment, their moment in the spotlight, to last forever. It was so perfect, so wonderful, that she didn't want it to ever end. They lifted their voices to sing the chorus, the choir harmonizing softly in the background.

Links in a chain,
We're bonded together.
Sharing a legacy,
That will last forever.

Day follows day,
Year trails after year.
We'll always stay close,
We'll always be near.

They were all bonded together, weren't they? Tehilla and her mother, Tehilla and Savta...and Tehilla and Henny. By opening her home to Henny, she'd learned to open her heart as well, and the Tehilla who stood facing the audience today was not the same girl who'd first memorized the words to this song a few weeks ago.

Eventually the notes wound down, and their voices along with it. The ear-crushing applause that followed accompanied Tehilla back to her spot on the stage. She could see that her mother was delighted and that Savta was clapping with all her might. She noticed her teachers smiling and saw Miss Brickstein mouthing to her, "Stunning!" Then she saw Henny walk off the stage, the glow on her face having nothing to do with the glare of the spotlights. And that, to Tehilla, meant more than anything else.

"Tehilla!" her mother said, gathering her in a tight embrace. "I had no idea… How'd you manage to keep this a secret?"

"That was something else, Tehilla," Savta said, shaking her head slightly. "You and Henny…your voices were just made to sing together."

Miss Brickstein passed by the table just then and swept Tehilla up in a hug.

"Some star, isn't she?" she remarked. Then she looked at Mrs. Markson. "I don't mean just her voice. The way she gave up her solo so Henny could have a chance to join the choir, and without telling Henny about it, too… Those two girls sounded absolutely stunning together, but I'm so impressed that it was all Tehilla's idea in the first place."

Mrs. Markson looked confused as she glanced from Miss Brickstein to Tehilla, who was blushing furiously. Suddenly, comprehension dawned as she hugged Tehilla again.

"Amazing, Tehilla," she murmured. "I'm so, so proud of you."

Savta smiled at Tehilla, and Tehilla reveled in the feeling of wholeness she felt right then. Her mind flitted back to a terrifying night only a few weeks ago, when she'd felt as if the ground was crumbling beneath her feet. She'd since regained her footing, and she was grateful beyond words that Savta was there that night, looking as gracious and healthy as always.

Mrs. Markson's cell phone jangled, and she turned aside to answer it.

"Hello? Oh, how are you? ...It really *was* beautiful... I'm so glad you were able to listen in... Such a wonderful surprise... Yes, here she is..." Mrs. Markson held out the phone to Tehilla. "It's Henny's mother," she whispered. "She wants to speak to you."

"Henny's mother?" Tehilla repeated, confused. Mrs. Markson put the phone in her hand. "Hello?" Tehilla said hesitantly.

"Tehilla!" came a warm voice. "That song you sang together with Henny was so beautiful. I'm so happy I was able to listen in."

"Thank you," Tehilla said politely.

"I heard so much about you from Henny," Mrs. Hart continued. "I wanted to thank you for being so welcoming to her. It takes such a load off our minds knowing that she's in such good hands — and that she has such a good friend." Tehilla didn't know what to say. Henny's mother didn't wait for an answer. "*Baruch Hashem*, Henny's father is doing much better. I don't know for sure how much longer we'll need to be away, but in the meantime, we are indebted to you!"

Tehilla finally found her voice. "We enjoy her, too," she said sincerely. She handed the phone back to her mother.

"I'll have Henny call you back later, okay?" Mrs. Markson said into the phone.

Henny disentangled herself from a group of choir girls and walked over to join the Marksons.

"You were absolutely magnificent," Mrs. Markson gushed, hugging the girl.

"You really were," Savta agreed, giving Tehilla a slight wink. The gesture chased away any pangs Tehilla might have felt, however faint.

"Come, girls," Miss Brickstein said, summoning the choir members to join her. "We're going to take a group picture now on stage."

Tehilla looked at her mother questioningly.

"Go," Mrs. Markson said, laughing. "We'll be right here when you're done."

Tehilla headed to the stage, with Henny right beside her.

Miss Brickstein handed her mother a camera before posing along with the group. "Smile, everyone!" Mrs. Brickstein ordered.

Devoiry, standing beside Tehilla, looped her arm over her shoulder. Tehilla hesitated for a moment, and then threw her arm over Henny. Then she faced the camera, smiling for all she was worth.